I0621206

SKINNY DIPPING DARE

a Camp Firefly Falls novel

ZOE YORK

All Rights Reserved
2016 Zoe York
ISBN-13: 978-1926527437 (ZoYo Press)
ISBN-10: 1926527437

CHAPTER ONE

Wyatt Henderson steered his rented 4x4 out of the small town of Briarsted and followed the signs toward Camp Firefly Falls. On the seat beside him lay the email from his SEAL teammate, Grady Mills. Short on details but rich in promise, the invitation to hang at a rustic camp in the middle of nowhere was exactly what Wyatt needed after the soul-sucking assignment he'd just come off.

He'd joined the SEAL teams to defend and protect American freedom. That commitment had never wavered. And now after a short-lived posting to the Pentagon, he was more eager than ever to get back to California. Return to a team that would be deployed overseas, hopefully sooner than later, and leave his temporary flirtation with the more political aspect of military leadership in the past where it belonged.

His mediocre performance review taunted him from where it sank in his bag in the trunk. It was the first in his entire career. This week of leave in the woods was exactly what he needed to ensure that when he did fly home, it wasn't with a chip on his shoulder. No internet, spotty cell service, and cold beer guaranteed every day. Add in the promise of fishing on a pristine lake and Wyatt was almost excited.

Almost.

He didn't do excited, not even for beer and fishing.

But it didn't sound awful. High praise inside his head right now.

He shook off the negativity, as much as he could, and focused on the drive through the climbing hills. He was west coast born and bred, but there was something quaint about the Berkshires.

Quaint and mosquito-filled.

He'd stocked up on bug repellent when he'd stopped at the outfitter shop in town. Bug spray, a new fishing rod, a camelback water unit that had been on sale, and two pairs of quick-dry cargo shorts. What passed for a shopping spree in his world.

As he crested yet another hill, he spotted the sign for the camp. He turned the corner and followed the narrowing lane through the gates and into a bit of a valley. A parking lot was the first thing he came to, and it was clear he'd be expected to leave his stuff here. A tent was set up on the far side of the lot, with a big-ass *Welcome* sign fluttering above it, but even from this distance he could tell it wasn't manned.

He glanced across the empty parking lot, then down at the email. He was a bit early for registration. Two hours. Better to be early than late.

He backed his truck into a parking spot along the perimeter and climbed out, surveying what he could see of the camp. The buildings all looked newly

4

painted and in excellent repair. This is where Grady went to summer camp? La-di-dah, Mr. Rockefeller.

Wyatt coughed as he swallowed yet another bitter thought. Jesus, he was glad this was a low-maintenance guys' week in the woods. The last thing he needed was for anyone to hear the negative shit in his head right now. He wasn't going to offend Grady or Danny Fox, the third guy in their three-man cabin. They'd just laugh at him and throw him in the lake.

But other people?

He hoisted his rucksack over his shoulder and grabbed his new fishing pole in his other hand.

Lord help anyone that got in front of him this week. Wyatt Henderson's filter was officially broken, and the only hope of it ever being repaired was a solid stretch of peace and quiet.

He strolled past the unattended registration tent and walked up to the main lodge. A sign on the door said they'd re-open after lunch, but before he could head back to his truck, he heard the buzz of a power saw from around the corner.

He found a tall, dark-haired man, maybe a little older than himself, working on what looked like the world's biggest treehouse behind the main lodge.

Wyatt cleared his throat and announced his presence. "I'm a bit early. Name is Wyatt Henderson. I'm staying here with two of my buddies for the next week."

The other man put down the power tool and sauntered over, holding out his hand. "Nice to meet you. Michael Tully. My wife Heather runs this place. I guess you figured out that nobody else is here to sign you in?"

"Sure did. I can just hang, if this is a problem."

"No problem. We aim to please. Let me grab your reservation details from the lodge and I'll show you where you're staying. Our last batch of campers left first thing, and my wife took advantage of the free half-day to do a team-building retreat for our staff this morning."

That sounded like the exact kind of fresh hell Wyatt had just left behind in Washington, so he kept his trap shut and nodded.

His home for the next week was the last cabin down a long path behind the main lodge. Remote and simple. There was even a hammock hanging on the wide porch.

Perfect.

"Appreciate this," he muttered as he dumped his bag on the steps and stretched his arms up to the sky.

Tully laughed. "It's the least I could do. I'll probably mess up the spiel anyway, so here's your information packet, and once your friends arrive, just head to the main lodge if you have any questions.

Dinner's at six, and there's a bonfire tonight."

"Thanks, man." Wyatt wasn't even listening anymore. He suddenly had plans—a date with the hammock to start. Then he was going to explore the trails behind the cabin, and find a remote access point to the lake. If all went well, tonight's dinner would be the only one he'd attend.

❋ ❋ ❋

Tegan's best friends were chattering back and forth about what they wanted to do first when they arrived at camp, but she wasn't really listening. Prina had offered to drive, which Tegan appreciated, because right now she was too excited to concentrate—on driving, or talking, or anything else.

It was kind of stupid, how much she'd emotionally invested in camp being totally awesome this week.

Except she needed awesome right now.

She was four weeks away from being homeless.

Eight weeks past being jobless.

If she hadn't already paid for this holiday—paid for it the second Heather Tully had opened registration for Retro Throwback Week and announced it in the Camp Firefly Falls Alumni Facebook group—she'd probably have backed out.

But she couldn't bring herself to email her

childhood friend and ask for a refund.

She didn't *want* to miss this. This week might be the emotional recharge she needed to figure out where she was going in life.

Or where she was going, period.

She needed to get out of New York. Even if she found another job, the last three years had taught her that Tegan and the Big City didn't mix well. She wasn't frugal enough to figure out how to save money and still have a life. And she wasn't urban enough to find a tribe in the concrete jungle, either.

Other than Prina and Molly, of course.

But Molly lived in Brooklyn and Prina spent more time flying around the world than she did in the city.

Tegan could move to Atlanta or Paris and probably see her bestie more often, because Prina's job as a news producer took her all over. And Molly could be convinced to move, maybe. That was high on Tegan's agenda for this week. Convince her other bestie to ship out of the city with her and start a hippie commune somewhere cheap as chips.

Molly could do her art there.

And Tegan…

Well, she could do something.

Anything.

God, she was desperate. But she needed to shove that thought away because camp was right around the corner.

Her heart thumped against her rip cage. Nervous all of a sudden—what if it wasn't amazing?—she tugged her hair out of the loose bun she'd shoved it into and re-did the twist.

Prina patted her on the knee, her eyes never leaving the road. "This is it?"

Tegan nodded. "Yep."

"Pretty drive."

"Yep."

"You need a beer when we get there?"

Molly laughed from the backseat. "Hell yep."

Tegan did need a beer. But as they drove through the camp gates, and she caught her first glimpse of the sun glinting off Lake Waawaatesi in the distance, she knew she needed something else first.

There were a few other cars in the parking lot. Most were parked close to the gate. Tucked off to one side, backed into a parking spot, was a giant SUV. She groaned to herself. Somewhere on the camp grounds was an anal-retentive blowhard with control issues.

That's the kind of assumption that got you into trouble at your last job. Well, she wasn't working this week. She'd work on assuming the best of people after she'd recharged the well in every other way.

Besides, she didn't think the worst of people who were awesome.

Like Heather Tully, who was sprinting across the parking lot, her arms waving in the air. "Tegan Bennett!"

"My favorite junior camp counsellor!" Tegan hollered back, racing to meet Heather. They hugged and spun around in a circle. "I can't believe you did this! Oh my God!"

Tegan was five years younger than Heather, but they'd clicked hard when paired together in Tegan's first year here, and remained buddies through the next three years until Heather outgrew camp. But they reconnected through the miracle of the internet age, and Tegan had been one of the first to join Heather's groups when the reimagined Camp Firefly Falls was still just a gleam in her eye.

And now it was a real-life gleaming beauty.

"I don't think this place ever looked this good when we were kids," Tegan said, gesturing at the main lodge, rising up behind the registration tent. "I'm so excited about this week."

"Me, too." Heather gave her another quick squeeze, then held out her hand and introduced herself to Prina and Molly. "So glad you guys could join us!"

"Is this the first week you've had original campers back?" Prina asked.

Heather nodded. "In a concentrated way, yes, although it's amazing the reach that the camp had over

10

the years. But this is the first dedicated week for alumni—and their friends, of course. Come on, let's get you registered."

It didn't take long, although Tegan's attention kept sliding toward the path down to the boathouse.

Heather clearly noticed, because she waved over a counsellor with a warm laugh. "We can take your bags up to your cabin if you want to head straight to the lake."

Oh yeah. Camp was going to be amazing. Tegan pulled off her t-shirt and shoved it in the side pocket on her backpack before handing it over to the super-cute-but-probably too-young-for-her staffer. "Last one in is a rotten egg!"

Both of her friends caught up to her as she hit the dock, and when she launched herself into the air, arms wrapped around her knees, ready to cannonball into the still, clear waters, she was taken back twenty years.

She hadn't had a career then, either. Her entire life had stretched before her, full of potential. So what if she was a couple years into her thirties and still didn't know what she wanted to do when she grew up?

Maybe she'd figure that out when she came up for air.

❉❉❉

Wyatt found himself whistling as he headed back towards his cabin. He'd tried the hammock, but the lake had called to him. So before Grady and Danny arrived, he'd headed off into the woods with his fishing pole and tackle box. A couple of hours of catch and release had done wonders for his mood.

Tomorrow he'd bring a cooler with him and not come back until he had dinner for his buddies.

Or maybe he'd take a sleeping bag with him and just not come back, period. A night under the stars sounded…well, it sounded like work, but in the good way. In the "damn, I miss the field" kind of way.

He rolled his neck, releasing the last bit of tension with a gentle crack of his vertebrae.

Camp.

Who'd a thunk it? What a great idea.

As the trees thinned around him and the sunlight grew brighter, he started to hear voices. He picked up his steps. It was beer o'clock, for sure.

But as he emerged into the clearing behind his cabin, he faltered, because it wasn't Danny's growly Chicago accent or Grady's smooth prep-school voice, either.

No, there were decidedly female gasps and shrieks coming from his porch.

"Wasn't that the absolute best?" said one of them,

and he came to a halt. This was awkward. Maybe if he waited, they'd go away.

"You were right. But oh my God, I need to put some clothes on before I freeze my butt off."

Or not. Were they naked? Maybe they didn't need to leave right away. Especially that one with the husky voice. He could think of a few things he'd like to hear her call the absolute best.

A third voice joined in the conversation. This one was oddly familiar, polished and smooth. She sounded like a female Grady. "We've only got fifteen minutes before craft hour, anyway. The schedule says they're serving vodka shots to go with the potato stamping. So let's hustle and get back there for that."

Craft hour? Vodka shots? *Potato stamping?*

Their voices dulled as they stepped into his cabin, and he rounded the corner, trying to recall if Michael Tully had said anything about craft hour.

He definitely had not.

What the everloving hell? And why were there three naked women in his cabin? Women who got giddy about potato stamping?

"These aren't our bags," the polished woman said, and he climbed the stairs.

He could see them now. Three women, all in variations of bikinis. The speaker was wearing a modest two piece. She was petite and pretty, with

13

dusky skin and straight dark hair. South Asian, probably.

A blonde in a much smaller bathing suit turned around, confusion painted all over her face. "Where are they?"

And then the second brunette, the tall, stacked one poured into a sports suit that was probably meant to be functional but still gave him blood-flow problems… she held up his rucksack one-handed, and that was a feat because he had everything but the kitchen sink in that thing. "This must be the boys' cabin," she teased, and her voice was like hot caramel poured over ice cream. "Oops."

There was something about her that put him on edge. The other two seemed harmless enough, but this one…she was brash and presumptuous and seductive. Like maybe she didn't give a fuck about boundaries or personal space. Like the next week would be a non-stop pajama party if he didn't put a stop to this nonsense right fucking now. He stepped into the doorway and tapped his hands against the frame, making his presence known. "Yeah. That's mine."

CHAPTER TWO

Tegan dropped the rucksack, narrowly missing her toe.

A giant man blocked the door. He was backlit, so all she could make out was that he was probably ten feet tall. Plus built like a GI Joe figure—broad shoulders, long torso narrowing down to tight hips, strong cargo-pant-clad legs that spilled into army boots.

A real-life action figure had just caught her breaking into his stuff. So she did the only thing that made any sense. She screamed and sprinted for the back entrance of the cabin.

Behind her she heard hysterical giggles as Prina and Molly followed her. She shoved her way out the back door and sprinted around the side of the cabin, but apparently GI Joe wasn't done with the conversation, because as they rounded the corner, he was sauntering down the front stairs with an "are you serious?" expression painted on his face.

She stopped and tried to catch her breath.

And started giggling again.

Well, it was funny. That he clearly didn't think so just made it funnier.

She took a deep breath, held out her hand, and tried to school her features. "Hi," she said breathlessly.

"I'm Tegan. We're your neighbours for the week, I guess." She squinted at the cabin ahead of them. "I thought we were in Nine, but must be in Eight."

He took a long, slow look at her outstretched hand. She didn't pull it back. She was brassing this out. *Yep, I touched your stuff, dude. And now we're going to be friends.* Or something. Neighbours for a week, at the very least.

Heat surrounded her fingers as he shook her hand firmly and she found herself squeezing back.

He broke off the handshake and crossed his arms over his very wide chest. "Might want to double check that it's your cabin for sure before you go rooting through some other guy's stuff."

"Right. Of course." She grinned. "Um, this is Molly and that's Prina."

He just nodded. So GI Joe didn't want to give his name.

"And we're in Cabin Eight. Maybe. We'll confirm that shortly." She backed up. "See you around."

"Maybe," he said, turning on his heel and stalking into his cabin. And just before the screen door slapped shut behind him, she was pretty sure she heard a muttered, "but not at fucking craft hour."

She frowned. Okay, so they probably wouldn't be friends. GI Joe was a buzzkill.

❊ ❊ ❊

16

Craft hour turned into cocktails before dinner, camp-style. Hard lemonade served in sugar-rimmed mason jars and beer in frosted glass mugs. It was entirely delightful, and from the way everyone was murmuring about the week's schedule, Tegan wasn't alone in being excited about the return trip down memory lane.

GI Joe didn't appear until shortly before dinner. He was flanked by two similarly built guys, a gorgeous black man who made friendly eyes at everyone — already an improvement — and a Scott Eastwood-clone who had a ready, practiced smile for Heather.

And a hug.

When the camp director squealed, "I missed you at registration! Do you remember Michael?" Tegan realized the Scott Eastwood clone was alumni, too. But if he knew both Heather and Michael, that probably put him a few years older than her.

Her attention swivelled back to GI Joe. Was he older than her, too? Maybe. Hard to tell. *And why do you care?* She didn't. She was just curious. Okay, she cared in a mildly intrigued by the grumpiness way.

"There's the guy from Cabin Nine. And he's got friends," Molly murmured. Maybe she hadn't noticed how Tegan had already been checking him out.

As the enemy, obviously.

All good camp weeks needed a nemesis, and GI Joe was a solid candidate. Her inner eleven-year-old approved.

"Hot friends," Prina said from the other side of her.

"Hot friends who are going to be living right behind our cabin," Molly said. She took a sip of her lemonade, licking the sugar from her lips. "I'm going to go introduce myself."

Tegan's inner eleven-year-old thought that was a terrible plan, but since she was actually a grown-up, she took a deep breath and followed, grateful that Molly bee-lined for the friendly one first, the guy who looked like Shemar Moore, right down to the panty-melting smile. He gave her a warm wink as his hand closed around hers. "I'm Danny," he said, his attention purely for Molly but his voice loud enough to make the introduction for everyone.

"Molly," Teegan's friend said with an eye-roll worthy purr. "And this is Tegan, and that's Prina."

He pointed over his shoulder. "Wyatt and Grady. Grady's the one who came here as a kid."

Molly gestured toward her. "Tegan, too."

Small talk. Not her forte. She gave a smile and a wave, but when Heather waved her over to introduce some of the other camp alumnus, she took the excuse —and grabbed another lemonade on the way.

By the time they sat for dinner, she was one vodka

shot and two hard lemonades past sober. Which was the only excuse she had for groaning out loud when their table assignment was half of a table—and the other half was occupied by cabin 9.

GI Joe, aka Wyatt, sat across from her. Prina was between them, on the end of the rectangular table, and Grady took the other end. Molly was between Grady and Tegan, and Danny say across from her, beside Wyatt.

None of them heard her groan.

None of them, except Wyatt.

He smirked to himself and even as her cheeks flamed with embarrassment, she thought, *yeah, that groan was completely justified, you jerk.*

"Tegan, Danny says you were a Firefly kid, too?" Grady asked from the far end of the table, and she jerked her attention to him.

"Yep. From when I was eight to thirteen."

"Did we overlap at all? My last year was 1993."

"That was my first year."

"Remember the long tables we had? And the meal line?"

She laughed. "And how starving we were by the time we made it to the tables, only to have to jockey for a spot to sit? This is way more civilized."

His lips twitched. "Our standards are higher now."

"I don't know. It might be fun to do that again one

night. Giant pot of chili being served out by the cook, grab your own bun and butter."

Danny reached for the tri-card menu in the center of the table. "Or we could have steak."

She laughed. "Or there's that."

Just then their waiter appeared—definitely different from the first version of Camp Firefly Falls—and Prina quietly reminded him that the three of them had ordered vegetarian meals for the week.

Tegan wasn't a vegetarian, but Prina was, and she hated that her bestie was often the odd person out. Molly agreed, so they'd all put down the veg option on their registration forms.

The waiter assured them the chef had an amazing set of choices for them, and pointed to the flip side of the menu Danny was holding. "Your options are listed there."

That was impressive. Usually there was one take-it-or-leave-it veggie meal.

Danny sighed as he handed over the menu. "No steaks for you?"

She winked at him and took a quick glance at the entrees. "Not when there's a portabello mushroom cap with my name on it," she said brightly.

Wyatt snorted and she dropped her smile. No wink for GI Joe.

She gave him a cool look instead. "Let me guess.

You think portabellos are un-American."

He paused a beat, his gaze holding hers, hot and piercing. He didn't want a wink from her anyway, that was totally clear. "Think whatever you want, lady."

"Name's Tegan," she said sharply.

She could practically feel him holding back an eye-roll from across the table, a hard, crushing judgement.

Fuck him and the macho train he rolled in on.

He just looked down at the menu and groused about something that she didn't catch. Wyatt from Cabin Nine wasn't going to play any part in her fun, relaxing week at summer camp. He was worse than a nemesis. He was a full-on party pooper.

❖❖❖

There was no dessert course with dinner, because Heather promised all the s'mores makings they could stuff their face with at the bonfire, and there would be snacks available later as well.

That was just fine by Tegan. Bring on all the things her inner eleven-year-old liked.

It didn't please GI Joe, though.

"I'm going to head back to the cabin," Wyatt said gruffly to his friends as the group moved en mass from the dining hall down to the bonfire pit.

She pretended not to hear. She didn't care. Good.

He should head back to the cabin. Leave the bonfire to the happy people.

"You can pull your old man early-to-bed routine the rest of the week," Grady said with a laugh. "But tonight we're going to toast to your return to the teams, brother. One beer. Come on."

A long pause, then a gruff, "sure."

Tegan picked up her pace. Well, if he was going to be there, she'd be sure she was sitting on the far side of the fire from him.

But that was easier said than done. Heather and Michael had done a masterful job of alternating "boys" and "girls" cabins, and already people were pairing up, or grouping up. Chummy all around, and there were only two logs left—side by side—when they arrived.

Probably what she deserved for eavesdropping on their conversation.

She sighed and sat down on the far end of the log, next to the guys from Cabin Five. They handed her the bag of marshmallows, and she took her first one. One of the camp counsellors came around with a tray of the other supplies—graham crackers and chocolate, both milk and dark—and another staffer circulated with sticks trimmed to the perfect taper for roasting.

What would Wyatt think—

"We don't even have to find our own sticks?" he joked, his voice full of contemptuous amusement.

Predictable. She rolled her eyes, and keeping her gaze on the crackling yellow flames, she lifted her voice. "Nobody said you have to have s'mores, GI Joe."

Silence reverberated around them.

Oh, shit. Had she actually said the nickname out loud?

Then he laughed, a rolling chuckle that didn't sound offended at all. Glamping bugged him but name-calling didn't.

Weirdo. Her lips twitched, and the conversations around the bonfire started again. Someone even started singing *Alice the Camel*, which made her twitch turn into a silent, body-shaking giggle, because another person chimed in, and before long, everyone around the circle was singing except Wyatt.

That made her happy.

She closed her eyes and took a deep breath, letting it out—letting it all out. The work shit and the money stress. Everything. *Out*. She was eleven again and back at camp. Friendship and adventure.

Sing-a-longs and s'mores.

Which reminded her…She blinked her eyes open and slid her marshmallow onto the end of her stick. The Cabin Five guys were way ahead of her, so she nudged the candy deeper into the flames, speeding up the browning process.

23

Brown, brown, brown...yoink! She grabbed it from the flames just as it started to char on the end, before it caught flames. Perfect.

Molly was licking chocolate off her fingers already. "So good," she mumbled around her mouthful of sticky sweetness.

"Right?" Tegan picked a nice piece of dark chocolate and pressed it into the pillowy softness of the hot marshmallow.

Even Prina was on her third piece of chocolate.

After savouring her first smore, she got another marshmallow ready to go. This time it was even more perfect, not even charred, and perfectly ooey-gooey in the middle. She stood up as she wiggled the marshmallow carefully off the stick.

It was perfect. Her mouth watered as she moved toward the tray of supplies.

Molly shrieked. "Oh, shit! Teeg, there's an ant on your marshmallow."

She jerked back, the sticky, delicious treat—meant for her, now being enjoyed by the tiny invader—still in her hand.

Wyatt laughed. "Afraid of a little protein, Vegan Girl?"

She glared down the line of logs. Of course he'd have something to say about it. "Don't be gross."

"Are you talking about the ant or the nickname?

Because you were the first to start with the latter. And the former is a perfectly acceptable source of protein. Speaking of which…don't marshmallows have gelatin in them?"

She rolled her eyes. "That would be a big deal if I was a vegetarian. Which I'm not, you dolt."

"More name-calling." He tsked. "What are you afraid of?"

An ant wriggling in her mouth. Obviously. "Nothing."

"Then do it. Make an ant-smore. Delicious."

"Stop it."

He laughed. "I dare you."

❊❊❊

What the hell was he doing?

He didn't give a fuck if she ate the ant or not. He shoved himself off the log so he was standing, too. "Never mind. Ignore me."

She cocked her hip to one side, her arm still outstretched. "You don't think I'll do it?"

"I don't think you need to. It was just something that came out of my mouth."

"Right, because you hate summer camp so much. We *all* know that, GI Joe, and you've only been here for like six hours." She scraped her teeth against her lower lip as her gaze flickered back and forth between him and the marshmallow.

Everyone else had fallen silent, again, and this time it was his fault.

Great. He was the fucking entertainment.

He shifted back on his heels. Best to get this over with, in that case. "I like a lot about this place." *Just not the people*, he added silently in his head. Although that Tully guy wasn't bad. And his wife seemed cool.

But this Tegan chick had attitude for miles. Like her legs, only more smart-alecky.

She held out her hand, her lips curving into an unexpected grin. "Do you like the ants?"

The question made him laugh. "Wasn't my dare."

The smile fell away and she swallowed hard. "Can I make it into a smore?"

He shrugged. "Sure. But no flicking the ant off in the process."

"You question my honour?" God, she was feisty.

He gave her a slow shake of his head, and maybe some of her amusement was rubbing off on him. "No."

"Good." She snapped her fingers and her friends shoved two graham crackers and a chunk of chocolate into her outstretched hand.

She was really going to do it. He watched in disbelief as she carefully pressed a piece of chocolate onto the marshmallow, then squished them between

26

the cookies.

Everyone was watching. He wasn't alone in being grudgingly impressed as she took a big bite, almost completely repressing her instinctive flinch. Only her eyes tightened as she quickly chewed, then swallowed, and did it again twice more until the ant-smore was all gone.

Shit. Danny clapped him on the shoulder as the entire bonfire circle cheered.

Tegan 1, Wyatt 0.

"Try harder next time," she said under the applause, and maybe he was the only one who heard her. He hoped that was the case. Because there wasn't going to be a next time.

The gorgeous hippie was bad for his blood pressure, and now he knew she was fearless to boot.

No, he was going to spend the next six days avoiding the hell out of her.

CHAPTER THREE

Saturday dawned bright and far too early.

Tegan frowned up at the cabin ceiling as she tried to figure out why she was awake. She rolled her head to the side, blinking the blurriness away as she focused her eyes on Molly in the twin bed closest to her, then craned her neck up to check on Prina. They were both still snoozing.

And it was barely dawn.

So why was she up?

Thump. Oh. There was something outside. Probably a raccoon. Silently, she slid out from under her blankets and padded across the cabin to peer out the front window. Nothing there.

She tiptoed back to the back door.

A ha.

GI Joe was awake. Of course he was. Probably thought sleep was for the weak or something like that.

She leaned against the wall and wrapped her arms around her body as she tried to figure out what he was doing. He was jumping from the ground up onto the porch of Cabin Nine. Up. Down. Up. Down. He did that at least ten times, then dropped to the ground and pumped out a bunch of pushups.

Oh, he was working out. She bit her lip and leaned forward. That explained the insane body. It had to be three and a half feet up to the porch, and he was jumping it with ease, both feet up. Down. Up...

Spying on him felt wrong, sort of. She should go back to bed. Breakfast wouldn't be served for another hour. She took a few steps away from the window, then moved closer again.

It didn't hurt to watch.

She was kind of like an anthropologist observing a new tribe. *The alpha male rises before the rest of the population and puts himself through a punishing routine of physical exercises.*

Now he'd moved on to a different pair of exercises. Some kind of tricep dip off the porch, lifting his legs, one at at time, so he was weirdly off-balance. Looked like he was making an already difficult exercise even harder, and at an insane pre-coffee hour. He alternated those sets with balancing his butt on the edge of the porch and crunching his knees in to his chest.

There was something beautiful about the quiet flow of his body through a workout he clearly knew by heart. She watched as his shirt front darkened with sweat, a growing vee that spoke to how hard he was working, and she found herself biting her lip, hoping he'd strip it off.

He was gruff and rude and he didn't even like her. Objectifying him...that was what was wrong with this situation. She shouldn't gobble up this secret glimpse at him when she wouldn't want him to know she was there, wouldn't want to get into the inevitable sparring that would follow.

Her pulse picked up as she imagined the conversation.

"Like something you see, Vegan Girl?"

"I told you, beefcake isn't my thing."

"You sure about that?"

Her face flamed. Holy shit, she needed help.

From behind her, Molly took a deep breath, then yawned. "Morning."

Tegan left her voyeur post and grabbed the printed out schedule for the day, then crawled back into bed, lying on her side so she could see her best friend. "Morning."

"What's on the agenda today?"

"There's yoga first thing. Then breakfast, followed by swim tests —"

Molly laughed. "They're really taking the retro throwback theme seriously, eh? Swim tests for adults?"

Tegan grinned and rolled onto her back. "It's a tradition. And it's way more than just testing one's ability to swim independently. It's also where you figure out your teams for the end-of-week swim meet."

"That sounds grossly competitive."

"It's fantastic."

"What do you want to bet the guys in Cabin Nine sweep all the races?"

Tegan made a face. Molly had a point, especially after the athletic display she'd just seen from GI Joe. "That can't happen."

"How exactly are you going to stop that from happening?"

Wyatt wouldn't know that the first four people to the raft would be named swim team captains. Grady would, and Danny might be in just for the friendly competition, but maybe they could be distracted. "I have a plan."

"Oh God."

"Don't worry, it doesn't involve you swimming at all."

"I like swimming," Molly protested. "Just not fast and in a crowd of insane, nostalgia-drunk campers."

"Never fear. I'll do the swimming part. You and Prina just need to keep Grady and Danny from the water long enough that they don't finish in the top two spots."

"Oh…" This time Molly's reaction was less protest-y and more conspiratorial. "That we can do."

Tegan grinned again. She was going to show GI Joe who was boss. Literally. He was going to be her swim team bitch.

✿ ✿ ✿

Wyatt went for a quick three mile run after his workout, then threw himself into the shower. Grady had given him a guilt-trip for his plan to hide in the woods, so he'd agreed to make an appearance at breakfast. The guys had already headed to the main lodge, but a quick look at the printed out schedule told him he still had forty-five minutes before breakfast. His gaze drifted down the paper. Yoga…pass. A *swim test?* No. Breakfast was happening, but not yoga or a swim test.

Just to make that clear to his well-meaning friends, he grabbed his fishing gear and took it with him to the dining hall.

The girls from Cabin Eight were just finishing up, and Wyatt ignored the irritating tug in his gut at the sound of Tegan's laugh. He leaned his fishing rod in the corner, then took his seat across from her. Her long, honey-colored hair was piled on top of her head in a floppy ponytail, and her face was clean and make-up free.

So the annoying woman was pretty.

So what?

He reached for the coffee carafe in the middle and roughly filled his mug.

"Cream?" she asked sweetly from across the table.

"I'm good." He cleared his throat. "What's for breakfast?"

It turned out he had his choice of waffles or a western omelette. He went for the eggs, which didn't disappoint. Meanwhile the conversation flowed around him. There was a weird undercurrent of something that he didn't quite understand—his own fault for missing the start of breakfast. Maybe Tegan had said something to piss off Grady or Danny, not that either of them looked annoyed, exactly. But they were definitely distracted.

As Wyatt's hunger receded, he took another look around the table. Tegan was wearing another athletic swim suit—the straps were visible at the neckline of her worn t-shirt. He frowned. "Is that an original Camp Firefly Falls t-shirt?"

She beamed at him. "It is."

Good Lord. Who kept a camp shirt for fifteen years?

"Do you have an old camp shirt?" Prina purred from beside him, but she wasn't looking at him—her question was for Grady, at the far end.

Wyatt's friend blushed.

A God damned Navy SEAL, and he blushed. What was going on?

Molly winked at Danny. "I bet there are shirts somewhere for sale in the lodge. Should we go on an adventure and find some? I'm feeling a little left out."

Wyatt snorted. Tegan's friends couldn't be more transparent.

Danny still fell for it. He grinned broadly. "For a pretty girl like you, absolutely."

When Molly blushed, Wyatt would have bet money it was forced. He shifted his attention back to Tegan, who gave him an innocent look. "Do you want to go on an adventure, too?" she asked, her voice lifting just a hair above the husky note he liked too much.

"I'm going fishing."

"Fun."

"No snarky comments about the innocent fish?"

She rolled her eyes. "And on that note, I think I'm heading down to the dock. Anyone else interested in re-living the swim test tradition?"

Danny and Molly shook their heads. Grady squinted like he was thinking about it, but then Prina said something about signing up for the tree-top walk — "if it's not too scary!", with a little gasp, too—and suddenly Grady needed to help her with that.

Well, if his friends were falling head-long into camp flings, maybe they'd stop giving him grief about fishing.

Swallowing the last sip of his coffee, Wyatt wished everyone a brusque good luck with their plans for the day, and grabbed his gear.

❄ ❄ ❄

Tegan waited until everyone was gone—Wyatt to his grumpy-man fishing hole, his friends distracted by *her* friends—and then she headed for the dock. Maybe a quarter of the campers had shown up, so it was enough of a crowd for her to feel competitive.

Heather hopped up on a stool and blew a whistle to get everyone's attention. "Okay, folks! By popular request, I reinstate the Camp Firefly Falls Swim Test! Same rules apply as when we were kids. You need to be able to tread water for two minutes, then swim to the raft and back. As a bonus, the first two swimmers to the raft are the unofficial swim team captains for the optional swim meet at the end of the week. If you want one of those two positions, be the first to the raft and grab either the red or blue teams vest."

She pointed toward the raft, where a counsellor stood in a lifeguard tank top. At his feet were two pieces of fabric, one red, one blue.

Tegan pulled off her t-shirt, then shucked her shorts, and started swinging her limbs to warm up.

The real trick to winning the race was being in the right position when treading water—far from the dock, closest to the raft, so when Heather blew the whistle at the end of the two minutes, you had a second head-start on the others.

"And remember, there might be some bumping in the race to the raft, so if that's not you thing, hang back and take it easy. But if you're in the fray, stay *hands off*. If Brandon on the raft sees any roughness in the water, he'll disqualify you. And his word is law. Understand?"

Everyone nodded and murmured their agreement with the rules.

"Then in you go!" She waved toward the water, and people jockeyed for position to leap in. Tegan waited, edging her way up the dock until most were in the water—and then she leapt wide, splashing into the cool lake water within the treading zone, but definitely one of the closest to the raft.

Off to a good start.

As Heather blew the whistle, signalling the start of the two minute treading, Tegan's arms and legs twisted through the water by rote. She slowed her breathing and thought about the times she'd done this as a kid. She'd never won the race. There'd always been a bigger kid, a bigger boy who was faster, who'd watched and plotted based on previous years. Was anyone else around her as intently focused on claiming this childhood victory? Or was she the only one channeling her inner pre-teen?

In her head, she was also trying to count down the two minutes. There wouldn't be a ten second countdown. The race would start, unexpectedly and with a flurry, once Heather blew her whistle again.

Maybe in fifteen, fourteen, thirteen seconds… Tegan exhaled, then inhaled. Six seconds maybe, if she'd counted right. Four, three —

The sharp whistle ripped through the air and Tegan dove under water, holding her breath at first, then exhaling in a controlled, slow stream as she kicked her legs hard and tried to get ahead of the pack. When she broke through the surface, she was neck-and-neck with a guy from Cabin Five.

Arms churning, legs strong, she motored toward the raft. There were people half a body's-length back of her, she could feel arms on either side of her legs, but the lake was clear ahead of her and she was gaining on the raft.

So was Mr. Cabin Five. Corbin? Calvin? She didn't care. He was her temporary foe, and he was going down.

It didn't go over her head that he was the second guy this week she'd turned into a nemesis. Although he wasn't anything like GI Joe.

No, Wyatt was in a category of his own. This other guy just represented a bunch of stuff in her head. Failure she didn't want to submit to. Competitions from the past. A need to reclaim her ability, maybe.

Wyatt wasn't a straw man for her to rail against. He got under her skin in a real way. *He* did, not just what he represented.

You've only had a handful of half-conversations with him.

She twisted her head to the side, sucking in a quick breath. Stroke, stroke, stroke, breathe. Stroke, stroke, stroke, breathe. Faster, harder she pushed herself, swimming away from whatever that random thought had been, away from the pack, until her hand slapped against the raft—and the soft cotton of a captain's pinnie.

Other hands scrabbled against the wood, and she pulled her precious prize under water, fisted in her hand, as she twisted around and headed for the dock again.

✿ ✿ ✿

Wyatt made it back to the main lodge in time for lunch. He caught Grady and Danny as they were leaving the cabin.

"What happened to the girls?" he asked, not because he cared in the least, but just to make conversation.

Grady frowned. "Prina bailed on the tree-top walk. Haven't seen her since."

"Molly disappeared right after we found our camp shirts, too." Danny said.

Wyatt frowned. "They ditched you?"

"I wouldn't say ditch," Grady said, pulling his phone from his pocket. "Wow, when they say no cell reception, they really mean it."

Danny's steps slowed. "Yeah, maybe they ditched us."

"No, really, Prina was totally into me. She just chickened out because she's not a fan of heights."

Wyatt scoffed. "You mean the journalist who reports from war zones and international sites of interest? That are often high up from the ground?"

Grady stopped and frowned, tucking his phone away. "She's not the reporter, is she?"

"She's the producer, man. She does everything the reporter does, and first. No way is she afraid of heights. And certainly not in the *'oh my, no, I could never!'* way I imagine she used to blow you off."

"Her voice didn't go up like that." Grady colored. "Well, maybe it did a little."

Wyatt swore under his breath. "What else was on the agenda for this morning that we missed?"

"We?" Danny's eyebrows hit the sky. "What do you care?"

"You were distracted on purpose," Wyatt growled. "This has the hippie's fingerprints all over it."

"The hot hippie with the endless legs?"

"Shut up." He stalked toward the dining hall. *And don't look at her legs.*

"I'm just saying, what does it matter?" Danny called from behind him.

That was an excellent question for which Wyatt had no answer. But it didn't matter. Whatever it was, he isn't going to let her win.

CHAPTER FOUR

Tegan leaned her hip against the counter in the Arts & Craft building and peered at Molly's handwork. "That's super cool."

From the far side of the counter, Prina pointed to the center of the silkscreen design. "Can you make the U look like a vulva?"

"Prina!" Tegan giggled. "Yeah, maybe, could you?"

Molly shook her head. "No. Also, stop using the word vulva, Prin. That's not going to catch on."

"Whatever. I'm just saying, make it super feminist-y."

Molly pointed her Exacto knife at the stack of bright pink t-shirts they'd bought in Briarsted that morning. "Think we've got that taken care of." Bending over again, she carefully shaved another bit of the blocked out design, then made a pleased sigh. "There. Done."

They looked down at the prancing unicorn surrounded by the words, *Magical Unicorns Unite!*

"Yes," Tegan said with a grin. "That's perfect. Now let's go get some lunch."

"I could just get started on the shirts…" Molly looked longingly at the large bottle of ink in the middle of the counter.

"Come on. Fuel first, then you've got the building

to yourself for the afternoon. Or with us, if you want help."

Molly wrinkled her nose. "I'd rather you spend the afternoon recruiting people to be on your swim team so we kick serious butt on Thursday."

"That's the spirit."

Their smug sense of accomplishment lasted exactly as long as it took them to get to the dining hall. Waiting outside, arms crossed against broad chests, frowns firmly in place, were three super soldiers. Or sailors. Tegan wasn't quite sure what Wyatt and company were, but they were definitely badass military—and she had a sinking feeling they knew she'd outsmarted them.

"Uh oh," Molly whispered from one side of her. On the other, Prina made an audible gulp.

"Hey guys," Tegan said with a brightness that was totally feigned. "What's up?"

"Heard you passed the swim test," Wyatt grunted. It was news to Tegan that words could even actually be grunted. Huh.

"Sure did."

"Also heard there was a bit of a competition there, too."

She shrugged. "Only for those that wanted to participate."

"Didn't even know about it. Shame it didn't come

42

up at breakfast."

"Well, you had your fishing stuff. You looked like you had a good plan for the morning already."

Grady cleared his throat and glared at Prina. "And the nerves about the tree-top walk? What was that?"

Tegan held her breath, but there was no need. Her bestie was a slick professional. Prina exhaled, an appreciative sigh, and she gave Grady a big smile. "I so appreciate you attempting that with me, of course."

He glowered. "Is your fear of heights a new thing?"

"I wouldn't say I have a fear of heights." She crossed her arms to match his stance and Tegan struggled not to laugh. "Maybe I'm allergic to men who assume I must be scared."

"You tricked me!"

"You were more than happy to play the savior." Prina rolled her eyes and waved to Molly and Tegan. "Come on, ladies. Our lunch won't eat itself."

Tegan was all set to lift her chin high and swoop past the men, but Molly messed up their grand exit by whispering an apology to Danny.

"What was that?" Prina asked incredulously as they hustled to their table, the men not far behind.

"Well, he's a nice guy," Molly protested.

"I thought you were on Team Tegan."

"I am."

43

"Then he's the enemy."

"Why, exactly?"

"Doesn't matter." Prina's voice was fierce.

Molly laughed. "You need food."

"Maybe."

They were all laughing as they settled into their now familiar seats—but the giggles faded as the guys joined them.

Molly kicked Tegan under the table.

She took a deep breath. "I apologize for not telling you there was an informal swim race this morning." She shot a quick glance at Grady. "Although it's tradition. You should have remembered if it was important to you."

He shrugged. "No big deal."

"What?" Wyatt protested. He fixed his dark glower on Tegan. "Yes, it matters."

"Why?" his friend asked from the end of the table. "All that's at stake is the captaincy of two made-up teams for a single activity on Thursday."

Tegan snorted. "Also known as the Camp Firefly Falls Invitational. The only swim meet held on Lake Waawaatesi."

"Invitational?" Wyatt asked. She didn't miss his incredulity.

"Only two teams can compete—the two captained by the winners of the swim test race."

His lips turned white. "And let me guess..."

She grinned. "Yep. I'm one of the captains."

His head swivelled like a bobble head at opening day of a baseball game. "Who's the other captain? I volunteer for all the races on their team."

She shook her head slowly. "'Fraid that's not how it works, GI Joe."

His eyes went wide. "What did you do?"

"I've already picked you for my team. Of course, it's optional. You can sit out. But if you want to race, you're racing for me."

"Your team."

She nodded.

He leaned back in his seat. "Well, it's a good thing I'm not that competitive."

You're such a pretty liar. She nodded. "Of course not."

They were interrupted by the waiter. Since none of them had even looked at the menus, the conversation faded long enough for them to make their meal selections.

When it resumed, it was Danny and Molly who talked, a little louder than strictly necessary, and they didn't stop until after the food arrived. Even then, every time Tegan opened her mouth to poke the bear —because it was irresistible, because he rose to the bait so nicely, because in an odd way, she liked the dark glitter of his eyes and the tightness of his sculpted mouth — she was stymied.

It was like nobody else enjoyed verbal sparring.

Except Wyatt. By the end of the meal, his knuckles were white where he gripped his cutlery, and when Danny cut her off for the third time, Wyatt dropped his fork against his plate.

Clatter.

"I didn't ask you to get in my face, you know."

She frowned at him. "Likewise."

He jerked his thumb toward Grady. "That guy promised me a week of fishing."

"I fail to see how that's my problem."

"You're like a moth to a flame with this shit, aren't you?"

"And you're a big dumb bear who can't help but stick his head in the jar of honey!" As soon as it was out of her mouth, she regretted it. For one thing, it didn't really work as a counter-analogy. For another, her voice was now well above anything that could be called talking-level. And it was never nice to call anyone dumb.

Even if he picked fights that drew the attention of the camp director.

"What's going on here?" Heather said as she approached, her voice friendly, but her eyes sharp.

"Nothing," Tegan mumbled.

46

Wyatt's jaw flexed, but he didn't say anything.

The camp director's gaze flicked back and forth between them. "You two are on kitchen duty."

"What?" Tegan protested as Grady howled laughter in the background.

"Fine," Wyatt said, shoving to his feet. "Just sign me up for a time slot she's not there."

"No can do," Heather said smoothly. "You two need to learn how to get along. Nothing a little dishwashing can't fix, I'm sure. Report to the kitchen as soon as you finish your lunch."

Tegan stood, too. "I'm done now. Might as well get this over with."

Wyatt glared at her. "Oh, are you long-suffering now? You've only known me for twenty hours."

"Twenty hours of being judged and name-called."

"You started that."

"That's nice," Heather said, making it clear that no, it wasn't. "Kitchen duty. Now. Go."

❖ ❖ ❖

She unleashed in him a raging, irrational beast. There was no other explanation for his behavior in the dining room. He needed to apologize…soon.

Wyatt didn't quite trust himself to open his mouth just yet.

So he stayed mute as the laughing kitchen staff pointed them to the washing station. Plunged his hands into the hot, soapy water and started scrubbing pots and pans like a bit of KP time might actually help.

He could feel Tegan's gaze on his back, her confusion pressing against his skin as if she actually touched him with her long, slender fingers.

Turn around and tell her this isn't the man you usually are.

He settled for clearing his throat and suggesting she dry.

"We can take turns scrubbing," she said softly as she took up a position at his right. "We were equally at fault for causing a disturbance. Maybe even more my fault for starting the whole thing this morning."

"I probably pushed you to that in some way." It was easier to admit than he'd thought.

"Did Grady really trick you into coming here?"

He shook his head. "Nah. Grady says 'camp in the Berkshires' and he means this. I just hear it as 'cabin on a lake'. Cultural difference, no malicious intent."

"Ah." She paused long enough to buff the last bit of moisture off a stock pot, then gave him a sideways glance. "Where are you from, then?"

"Wisconsin. Farm boy. Summer vacation was spent doing chores, not learning how to row."

She laughed gently. "Not everyone who came here

as a kid was Richie Rich."

"Is that a reminder that I shouldn't assume anything about your own background?"

"Something like that."

"Noted."

Another pause, another pot dried. "I'm from New York. Not the city. Upstate. And my father paid for me to come to Camp Firefly Falls for two weeks every summer instead of having me to come to visit him—in the city. Now I'm twenty-nine and I live sixteen blocks from him, and I haven't seen him in eight years."

"That sounds complicated."

"A fact my mother reminds me of on a regular basis." She laughed again. This time it wasn't that gentle. Like she needed to find it funny because the alternative was too sad.

"She's not in the city?"

"Very much not. She's…well, not a farmer, exactly. Not like you'd recognize, anyway. But she's got a few acres just outside a small town, and she makes soap."

"Ah. So that's where the hippie genes come from."

"Both of my parents. My father may be a ruthless business man, but he wears Birkenstocks."

"And what do you do?"

She wrinkled her nose. "I worked for an insurance company. Nothing that exciting, but their headquarters are in Manhattan, so when I interned in their communications department during college, I realized they might transfer me there at some point."

"Good plan." He handed her a small frying pan. The stack of dirty stuff to his left was dwindling fast.

"It was. Until I was laid off."

"Ouch."

"Yeah. Anyway, enough about me."

"Why?"

"Because it's depressing and this week is supposed to be about having an awesome experience. I need awesome right now. Not a retread on how much my life sucks."

He winced. "And I haven't been helping on the awesome front, huh?"

"Nothing to do with you. It's all on me." She gave him another sidelong glance, this one curious and lingering. "Can I tell you something embarrassing?"

"Definitely. Embarrassing secrets have a way of bonding enemies." He winked at her.

"Good," she whispered, leaning in. "Because one thing that was kind of awesome was watching you work out this morning."

He didn't know what he'd been expecting, but it wasn't such an obviously flirty secret. And the punch of awareness was a surprise, too. Hello, Vegan Girl. "You watched me?"

"For a while."

"You should have joined me."

"You'd have bitten my head off."

Yeah, probably. A lot had changed since he'd started washing the pots. "Sorry about that."

"Meh. Water under the bridge." She reached for the pan he'd just finished washing and their fingers brushed, slick from the water, an easy slide that was far too brief. "Are you really serious about it? The other guys weren't out there with you."

"They're in better shape than I am. Or rather, I'm getting back in shape, and they're on a rest day."

She gave him a disbelieving look. "Right. Because you're such a slacker."

"I was on a desk job for the last three months. I'm heading back into a more active role and I need to hit the ground running."

"Or climbing," she said dryly.

"Pretty much."

"So you're military."

He nodded.

"I probably shouldn't have called you GI Joe mockingly."

"I've been called worse."

"I'm sorry."

"Don't be. You meant it. It was even kind of funny."

"About as funny as you calling me Vegan Girl?"

51

He laughed out loud. "Yeah. Almost that hilarious."

"So are we calling a truce?"

"Sure." He reached for an oversized mixing bowl, the second last dish they had assigned to them. "I'll even be on your swim team."

"Music to my ears," she murmured, and his gut tugged painfully.

What was he getting himself into?

And when was the last time he'd ever gone so far off plan?

CHAPTER FIVE

Molly missed dinner that night, but she reappeared at the girls' cabin as Tegan and Prina were putting on long-sleeved tops for the bonfire. The day had taken an unseasonable turn towards cool, which made the bonfire all the more appealing, but the walk there and back would require layers.

Tegan was mid-yawn when their friend burst through the front door, pink t-shirts waving in her hand like a pom-pom.

"They're done!" Molly exclaimed. "No yawning. Stop that."

Tegan laughed. "Yay. And sorry. I'm suddenly exhausted."

"Well, no kidding. You've spent the entire day flirting with the angry man next door."

"Flirting?" Tegan snorted. "Try avoiding."

"Yes, you should *try avoiding* him. That would be a great first step," Prina teased from her bed.

"I am." And she had been—after they finished the dishes, he disappeared and she headed to afternoon yoga, where she knew there'd be zero chance of running into him again. But even as she said it, a picture of him sitting at the far end of the Cabin Nine log at the fire popped into her head, and she found herself trying to think of conversations that might draw him out of his shell.

Not that he was shy. No, not at all. But guarded, absolutely. And after their conversation this afternoon, she had a new appreciation for some of the reasons why.

"You're thinking about him right now."

"I am not."

Molly wiggled her finger at Tegan's forehead. "You're frowning. That's a Wyatt line right there."

"See? He makes me frown. Not flirt."

Prina leapt to her feet. "A ha! So you were thinking of him."

Tegan rolled her eyes. "Let's go."

Molly waved the shirts in the air. "Do you want to wear one?"

Tegan reached for them. There were three different sizes in the bunch Molly had brought back from the Arts & Craft building. She tossed a small over to Prina, then held up a medium and a large, trying to decide which would fit her better.

The large was pretty big.

Man-sized, even.

She snapped her fingers at Prina. "Hold on. Wait."

"What?"

They'd called a truce. So why did she want to trick Wyatt into wearing the shirt?

Maybe it was about fairness. He'd dared her, she

needed to dare him back. Or maybe she wanted to prove to her friends that she wasn't flirting with anyone—wasn't thinking about him in any way other than as her nemesis.

So what if she knew he had a soft side, and they had a shared secret about job worries?

He could handle a little tease.

And if he couldn't, then it was his loss. She was back on track and focused on having fun this week.

❊ ❊ ❊

He almost passed on the bonfire. But he'd skipped dinner, heading into Briarsted on the pretense of needing a new lure, and then he stayed there, grabbing a diner meal so he didn't have to face Tegan across the dining room table.

He'd felt bad about that, and his burger had tasted like sawdust as he swallowed it down.

So he wasn't going to stay away tonight. He might even eat a s'more. He'd draw the line at singing in the round, that wasn't going to happen, but he could nod his head or something.

Grady and Danny were nowhere to be found when he returned to the cabin. Assuming they were already at the bonfire, he quickly dropped off his purchases from the outfitter and headed back down the path—

only to realize the women from Cabin Eight were ahead of him.

His pulse picked up as he watched Tegan run her fingers through her hair, shaking it loose from where it had gotten caught on the neck of a long-sleeved shirt she'd pulled on. The shirt was long, skimming the tops of her legs, and her shorts almost disappeared under it.

Heavy, unexpected lust pulsed through him at the thought of her naked except for that shirt.

Or any shirt, really.

Maybe *his* shirt. No shirt at all.

His steps slowed further. He didn't want them to notice him just yet. He wanted to watch her, hear her laugh, and imagine that sound turning to a hitching gasp as he tossed her onto a bed.

That got his dick's attention. God, what would she be like in bed? The give and take of their verbal sparring suddenly took on a filthy, foreplay tint. The next time she called him GI Joe, he could crowd closer, push against her and make her eyes spark for an entirely different reason.

But she wouldn't, because they'd acted like adults and come to an understanding.

He broke into a jog, not caring that his footsteps were heavy and would draw their attention. He wanted Tegan's attention in more ways than one. "Vegan Girl!"

She spun around, a grin spreading across her face. "GI Joe."

He grinned right back. "Heading to the bonfire?"

"Sure am." She glanced down at her hands, and he caught a flash of pink. She shoved it in Molly's oversized bag, and waved off her friend's protest. "Later."

"What's going on?" he asked as he fell into step beside her, her friends ahead of them a few feet.

"It's a long story. Perfect for the bonfire. What did you end up doing this afternoon?"

"Went into town."

"Ah."

He cleared his throat. "Bought a new lure."

She looked across at him and winked. "Excellent sharing."

His arm swung loose between their bodies, his hand itching to take hers—what the hell?—so he shoved both fists into his pockets and shrugged. "Trying to be social."

He got a slow, appreciative smile in return and something unfamiliar fluttered in his chest.

Being a grown-up was feeling pretty dangerous at the moment. So he cleared his throat again and changed the subject. "So how does this swim meet work, anyway?"

"We only do one length, to the raft and back.

Freestyle, backstroke, butterfly, breaststroke. There as many heats as we have people wanting to race, and then we do semi- and quarter-finals."

"Too easy."

She huffed a sharp laugh.

"It's just a saying."

"That reflects your cocky attitude."

He shrugged. She wasn't wrong.

"Well, bring your A-game and I'll forgive the cockiness."

"Yes, captain."

They met Grady and Danny just before the bonfire. Wyatt was laughing at something Tegan had said, so he may not have acknowledged his friends' presence. But he sure as shit heard Grady lean over to Prina and mutter, "What is happening?"

Prina put her finger to her lips and innocently batted her eyes as Wyatt glowered at her. "Shhh. Just sit back and enjoy the show."

"There's no show." Tegan gave Wyatt a hip bump. He didn't move, but inside, he liked it. A lot. "We sorted out our differences, realized we have more in common than we thought, and he's agreed to swim on my team."

"Exactly," he said gruffly. "All's well that ends well."

Grady gave him a suspicious look, but then Cabins

Five and Three arrived and the crowd shifted them toward the fire.

Molly and Prina sat on their log, closest to where Grady and Danny were sitting. Leaving one seat on the far side of Danny and the other on the far side of Prina.

He frowned. But what could he say? *Move your asses down so I can sit next to Tegan*? No, he wasn't ready to declare interest like that. Not publicly. So he sat on his log and she sat on hers, four people between them.

He nodded his head to a few songs, and made a few s'mores.

It was tolerable, because the whole while, he got to watch her. Her wide, easy smile. Her bright eyes. Her voice, gorgeous and light. How had he missed how well she could sing the night before?

She was…lovely. Kind and fun.

Wyatt was a lot of things—strong, capable, reliable. But he wasn't fun. Hadn't been for a long time.

He had no right lusting after someone so lovely. He should head to bed, since he had to be up early. Tomorrow was a long run day.

It took him another ten minutes to force himself to stand, and when he did, Tegan's head jerked up. "You leaving?" she asked, like it mattered.

His chest tightened. "Yeah. Early to bed and all

that."

She nodded, her gaze just for him. "Wait a second. I've got something for you."

He moved closer, ignoring the curious looks from his cabin mates. They could mind their own fucking business.

"We made…well, that is, Molly made…" She stood and laughed a little to herself. "Team t-shirts. For the swimming team."

"Team t-shirts?"

"Molly found silk screening equipment in the craft building and we hit up the art supply store in town."

The flash of pink. "Let me guess…"

She gave him a rueful smile. "You saw a glimpse of it earlier."

He groaned. "No."

She leaned over and pulled it out of Molly's bag. Extra pink. And it didn't even look like it would fit him. He'd be squeezed into it like a sausage casing. "So…yeah." She narrowed her eyes. "I dare you to wear this all day tomorrow."

Huh. Still lovely. But her sweetness had a sharp edge to it.

He wasn't sure which he liked more.

So he nodded and took the shirt. No way was she winning this one. Time to even the score.

＊ ＊ ＊

Sunday dawned just as early as Saturday had. Tegan rolled over and buried her face in her pillow in a desperate attempt to chase sleep down, but before she could drift off again, she heard him.

Thump thump thump. Faster than yesterday morning. Three thumps, pause, three more. He was running up and down the steps of his cabin, she was pretty sure.

She resisted the urge to get out of bed and go watch.

That didn't stop her cheeks from flaming as she imagined the flex and twist of his body as he pushed himself through a workout.

And when the thumping stopped, and nothing replaced it, she felt an unexpected ache of disappointment. He was gone. She didn't need to get out of bed to know that, but she did, and as she peered out the window into the early dawn quiet between the two cabins—devoid of GI Joe—the loss of the opportunity sliced straight through her.

What opportunity? The night before they'd been friendly, but nothing else. And he'd headed to bed shortly after accepting her dare.

Well, that was one legit reason to be looking for him.

Was he wearing the shirt?

He'd taken it, his fingers brushing hers in the process. Then he'd jammed it into a pocket on his cargo shorts and turned his attention back to the fire.

"Is it breakfast yet?" Molly grumbled from the next bed.

Tegan pushed off her blanket and swung her legs out of bed. "Yep."

"There's something in the air up here. I'm constantly starving."

"I think it's called exercise."

"I have a physical job!" Molly reached for the sky and groaned as something cracked.

"That doesn't involve hiking or swimming or even yoga first thing. Speaking of which…"

"Are we going to that?"

"Yep." Since Wyatt wasn't around—and she'd taken the long way around the cabin, peering out the window to double-check—she might as well get her bending on. She picked up the day's itinerary.

7:30 am… yoga

9:00 am… rope climbing at the obstacle course

11:00 am… craft hour — macrame owl wall hanging *perfect to take home to your mom!*

1:00 pm… kayaking

3:00 pm… nature hike

9:00 pm… drama club performance at bonfire

The way the camp program worked, if there wasn't something organized that appealed to you, you had free run of the camp. Swimming, hiking, crafts, canoes from the boat house and the world's best variety of board games in the main lodge.

But that didn't help her figure out where Wyatt might spend the day. Nothing on the list sounded like his kind of fun, and she didn't know where his fishing hole was.

Besides, what kind of dare success would it be if he just wore the pink shirt *fishing*? Alone?

She'd keep her eyes open, and if need be, send Molly and Prina into the enemy camp to gather intel.

CHAPTER SIX

Without a cell signal, Wyatt couldn't be sure how far he was going on his morning run. He should have bought a GPS unit at the outfitters. So to be on the safe side, he pushed past his usual ninety minute long-run time and kept going to the two hour mark.

His lungs and legs were long past the burning point. Everything was flowing like the trained machine he was, but he knew he needed to stop sooner than later if he wanted to be in any shape to do it again the next day.

Plus it was time to put on Tegan's pink shirt and parade through camp.

He sprinted back to the cabin, using the last of his reserves, then dropped in the shower and sat there, his mind blank and his body perfectly achy.

Eventually he reached for the soap. Then he stood. And when he emerged, clean and refreshed, he pulled on the shirt.

It didn't matter that it was just a hair too small.

Or that it had a unicorn on it, prancing through the waves.

She'd dared him. Hell, he'd have worn it anyway. He knew the power of team spirit. But this was a dare, and Wyatt Henderson *never* backed down from a dare.

He wore that fact like a badge of honour. Right on top of his hot pink unicorn tee.

He also pulled on black gym shorts and shoved his feet into flip flops, then headed down the path, his attention immediately pulled to Cabin Eight. Nobody was home there. All the cabins were empty. Everyone else was doing whatever was on the schedule today, or something schedule-adjacent.

So he forced himself to head through the woods to the obstacle course area.

He'd thought the last thing he wanted was to spend any time with wannabe Rambos. But it turned out that mooning around like a lovesick teen was even worse. Time to do some rope climbing.

❀ ❀ ❀

By mid-morning, Tegan hadn't seen Wyatt, and she was...grumpy about that. Damn it, his attitude had imprinted on her somehow.

Jerk.

And the worst part of it was that her roommates noticed.

"Why don't you go ask Grady where he is?" Prina said as they left the rope-climbing instruction session —because seriously, that was never happening—and headed for the docks.

"Where who is?" Tegan asked, but it came off petulant and not believable in the least.

After they did a quick spin in kayaks from the boat house out to the raft and back, she busied herself with returning the paddles and hanging up their life jackets just so.

Molly didn't let that stop her from picking up where Prina stopped. "Maybe we should fly a Team Tegan banner up the flagpole. Call a team meeting so he appears."

He wouldn't come. He'd swim for her, but that was it. She glared at her now soaked shorts. She should have stripped them off before going kayaking. "I'm going to get changed before craft hour."

Neither of her friends took the hint, and even though they weren't as wet as her—had she been paddling that furiously?—they followed along as if they too needed to change.

"Don't be grumpy, Tee," Molly said as she stomped into their cabin.

"Okay."

"We get it," Prina added, stretching out on her bed.

Tegan stripped out of her wet clothes, deemed her swimsuit dry enough, and pulled on a new pair of shorts. "Get what?"

"He's your camp crush."

"Don't be ridiculous."

"Next thing you know you'll be looking for him everywhere you go. Sneaking up to the loft above the music hall and holding hands for hours as the warm afternoon sunlight streams through the window."

Tegan narrowed her eyes. "What?"

"Nothing." Prina's cheeks turned pink. "I may have had a camp crush of my own once upon a time."

"There's no music hall here. No loft. Not happening."

"Sure."

"Stop it. Ready to go? We're doing arts and crafts at the top of the hour." She headed for the cabin door, wanting to be out of this conversation as soon as possible. "I'll wait on the porch."

"Looking for him everywhere you go!" Prina called.

"Hardly," Tegan muttered to herself as she stepped outside. "I'm just excited about the macrame owl wall hanging."

❊ ❊ ❊

Wyatt ignored the ribbing Grady and Danny were giving him about tearing up his hands on the rope.

"I wasn't showing off," he muttered as he poked at the biggest blister.

"Right..." Grady drawled. "So you don't want me

to get the first aid kit?"

"Fuck off." He didn't need anyone playing nurse to him. "I'm going to go rack out for an hour before lunch. I'll doctor up my own injuries, thank you very much."

He waved as he turned away from them and headed down the path toward the cabins.

The door to Cabin Eight swung open as he was rounding the bend, and Tegan stomped out, muttering something about an owl.

He raised his hand, but she didn't see him right away. Which was for the best, because his hand was a torn-up bloody mess.

Sticking it behind his back, he raised his voice. "Hey there."

She jerked around from where she'd just leaned against the porch post. "Oh. Wyatt." She grinned. "Nice shirt."

He glanced down. "I got a bit of blood on it, sorry."

"What happened?" She gave him a look of alarm as she hurried down the steps.

He pointed to the streak of red at his hip. "Nothing. I just...my hands. Nothing a bit of antibiotic cream and a bandage won't fix."

She gasped as she took his hand in hers. "These look bad."

"They're fine."

"Let me…" She pulled him toward her cabin, pointing to the steps. "Sit here."

He sat. She rushed past him, returning quickly with a small, store-bought first aid kit. The bandages in it wouldn't stay stuck to his hands, but he let her crack it open and carefully clean his hands.

Behind him, the screen door creaked open again, and Tegan's cabin mates carefully picked around them.

"We're off to craft building, Tee," one of them said, but Wyatt wasn't sure which one because his attention was locked on Tegan's fingers as she dabbed Polysporin on each bit of broken skin.

She nodded and mumbled something unintelligible, which they accepted.

Wyatt held his breath as she slowly rolled on bandages, then repeated the entire process on his other hand, where he just had one blister on his thumb.

"There," she finally said under her breath. "All better."

She was kneeling between his legs, one of her knees on the ground, the other bent in front of her. He reached for her arms, carefully using the tips of his fingers to press her up onto her feet.

He stood, too.

"Thank you," he said gruffly, and she blinked up at him.

"Of course."

He lifted his hands in the air. "I promise these won't interfere with the swim on Thursday."

She gave him a weird look, then nodded. "Good."

"So...crafts?"

"Yeah. A wall hanging we can take home to our mothers."

He laughed. "Maybe I should come along and make that."

"Where were you headed?"

"Oh. Um, back to my cabin. Fix these up and have a nap before lunch."

"Ah."

"Maybe I'll do that still."

"Okay."

Their conversation had suddenly gotten awkward, and he frowned. "Okay."

She frowned back. "See you at lunch, then?"

"Sure."

He watched her head down the path, confused about what had just happened.

One thing was sure, though. He didn't mind Tegan playing doctor for him. Not at all.

❊ ❊ ❊

Tegan moved through the rest of the afternoon in a confused daze. She went back to the docks after lunch for more kayaking, this time with an instructor, but the entire time she was painfully aware of the three guys — well, one guy and two wingmen — kicking back in the Adirondack chairs halfway up the hill.

That awareness kept her off-kilter through dinner, and she skipped the bonfire, opting to head back to her cabin to try and get an early night's sleep instead.

The Land of Nod was not that easy to visit.

Even after her friends quietly crept in and settled down for the night, rest evaded her, and finally, once Molly had started lightly snoring and Prina had been still for a good long while, she crept out of bed and headed outside to stare at the stars.

In all her excitement over *doing* stuff at camp, she'd forgotten how much she liked that camp sometimes forced her to slow down and do nothing.

And doing nothing in the middle of nowhere had a pretty incredible canopy at midnight.

"Wow," she breathed as she spun in a slow circle, taking in the clear expanse of sky and the million stars that decorated it, seemingly just for her.

"Can't sleep?"

Tegan jumped at the quiet question rumbled from the darkness. Or not just for her. Even as her pulse hammered at the base of her neck, she knew it was anticipation and not fear that was driving her immediate, visceral reaction. She straightened up.

71

"Nope."

Wyatt stepped out of the shadows and gave her a slow up and down. "You need some warm milk or something. What do vegans drink when they've got insomnia…warm almond milk? Or is that cruel to almonds?"

She rolled her eyes. "I ate an ant. I'm obviously not a vegan."

"That was a dare."

"Is that how your principles usually work? Wiped away by a stupid dare?"

He didn't answer right away. The night sounds of the forest behind them filled the silence of his non-reply, and she shoved to her feet. Not her problem if he couldn't handle a little criticism.

She waved her hand. "Well, I'm going to bed."

"No." He cleared his throat. "That's not how my principles work. I apologize. And I don't think that's true for you, either. I've been a jerk."

Sometimes. She sighed. "You've also been a good sport."

"Unexpectedly so?"

"You know what?" She licked her lips. "I honestly don't know what to expect from you. You're an enigma. That first night you were so grumpy, and you growl when I push your buttons, but you're really not a bad guy."

"Is that two compliments in a row?"

"Not sure how to handle it?"

He grinned, a flash of white in the quiet darkness. "I'll manage. Wanna tell me what's on your mind, why you can't sleep?"

"No teasing?"

"Cross my heart."

She shrugged. "It's always like this. Get a few days into camp, and you discover something you really like, and then the week ahead suddenly doesn't seem long enough."

It was a lot of honesty. Too much, probably. Because she wasn't talking about the swim team or crafts. Her heart hammered in her chest as the words echoed around her.

"Well, this is my first time at camp," he said slowly, not looking at her. "But I appreciate you telling me that. So I know I'm not crazy."

Relief washed over her, cool and slick. She nodded. "Normal. At least for me. Although everyone else seems to be sleeping just fine."

He moved closer, his gaze flicking over her enough to make her skin prickle with awareness. "Maybe they haven't found something they like enough to keep them up at night."

"Their loss."

"You're not complaining?"

She shook her head, suddenly mute.

"Even with the countdown. That in a few days we head in different directions." He paused, his voice rasping to a halt. She held her breath, but again he moved away from naming *them* as the thing they were talking about. "And leave this place behind."

She swallowed around the lump in her throat. "Even then. It might just be a few days, but it's still an amazing experience."

He gave her a long, hard look that made her want to melt. "We talking about swimming?"

She shook her head. *No.*

"Macrame?"

No.

He was right in front of her now, big and warm. Heat radiated off his solid body and she breathed in the scent of him for the first time. He'd showered after the bonfire. Soap and clean, scrubbed skin. But there was a hit of smoke, maybe on his shirt, and he smelled like everything she'd ever wanted.

In a few days they'd head in different directions.

He'd said it out loud, like he was warning her.

She lifted her hand, moving slowly, like reaching to touch him was an out of body experience. He exhaled audibly as her fingers wrapped around the loose edge of his flannel shirt, then his hand was around the back of her neck, his fingers thick and warm against the

74

skin beneath her hair. His thumb traced down the column of her throat until he found her pulse.

He groaned.

Deep and surrendering. She'd never forget that sound as long as she lived.

Then his lips were on hers, featherlight at first. A brush, a caress, a whisper of unrestrained need. She tipped her head up, giving him more room to play, and he pressed deeper. Harder, turning the kiss into a bruising demand.

More.

She tugged him closer and his free hand found her hip. Yes. He held her against him as his lips quested ruthlessly. This was a kiss that might never end, she thought dimly. Good. If it never ended, they'd never have to talk about how it might be a bad idea.

When she breathed in next, maybe she parted her lips, or perhaps he pushed them open. It didn't matter who started it, because Wyatt took over.

Her heart raced as he slid his tongue inside her mouth, taking the kiss from hot to filthy in the blink of an eye. He was consuming her now, his hands tightening his hold on her body as he swallowed her moans. She slid her hands lower on his torso, finding the edge of his t-shirt.

The skin on top of his abs was warm and taut, pulled tight over a ridged terrain she wanted to explore up close and in depth. The muscles clenched against her touch and she stroked higher, emboldened by his reaction. She was flying, full of adrenaline and something else, something unfamiliar but exciting.

Kissing Wyatt was insane and intense, but completely right.

He eased out of her mouth, and she whimpered against his lips as she squeezed the hard planes of his back. "No..."

"Not here." He was breathing hard, and he pressed his forehead against hers. "And we both have cabin mates."

"It's okay," she whispered, feeling sluggish and hungry for another hit of Wyatt.

"I've got an idea." He licked along the edge of her lower lip, then pressed an endearingly sweet peck at the corner of her mouth. "Do you like ice cream?"

She pulled back, searching his face with her gaze. "What are you thinking?"

"It wouldn't be camp without secretly raiding the kitchen in the middle of night, don't you agree?"

CHAPTER SEVEN

Who the hell thought shared cabins were a good idea? Wyatt wanted to find a private room—with a king-sized bed—and figure out just how much Tegan liked kissing.

Among other things.

The other things would have to wait. But more kisses could definitely happen at the main lodge.

He took her hand in his and they ran together, shadows flitting through even darker shadows, and as they neared the main buildings, he tugged her off the path and around to the back near the kitchen.

"This door's lock is busted," he whispered. "Fixing it is on Michael's so-called 'Honey Do' list, but Heather wants her treehouse built more, so…"

Tegan laughed quietly when he pulled it open. "I think this lock has been broken since before my time at camp."

"Damn it," he whispered as they crept down the hallway toward the kitchen. "I thought I was showing you something special."

She reached out and grabbed his arm, pulling him close as she pressed up on her toes. "You are," she breathed, then kissed him hard and fast, right on the mouth. "Thank you."

"Don't thank me until I successfully get you ice

cream," he growled as he lifted her up and pressed her against the wall.

"Maybe I don't care about that," she panted, wrapping her legs around his waist, urging him closer.

He slapped his hand against the wall and erased any space between their bodies. He didn't care either. She was warm and soft and so damn sweet it hurt not to kiss her.

So of course someone flipped on a light at the far end of the hall. Another room, not the dining room or whatever lay beyond it, but close enough to cast a pale glow through the door.

Tegan froze, her mouth on his neck.

All his instincts kicked into high gear. He mentally retraced their steps back toward the door. There was a closet back there. If it wasn't open, they could get back out the broken door, but that was the wrong direction from the ice cream he wanted to lick off her body.

So he wrapped one arm under her lush bottom and the other tight around her waist, and sprinted for the kitchen, moving through the swinging door like a two-headed ninja. He set her down and pointed to the far side of a stainless steel island before catching the door on on the swing back, freezing it before it could squeak again.

Heather Tully giving them kitchen duty had been a gift. He'd already been in this space, and knew it well enough to navigate in the dark. His eyes had already adjusted, so he moved quickly and silently to where she waited, and pulled her into his lap.

No sense wasting the cover of darkness.

She opened for him willingly and he lost himself in the taste and feel of her mouth until endorphins replaced adrenalin, and they didn't need to keep each other quiet any longer.

Then he kissed her again, just for the hell of it.

"Why didn't we do that the first night we met?" he finally muttered when she rolled to the side and giggled into his shoulder.

"Good question," she said with a sigh. "Should we head back to the cabins now?"

"What?" He pulled his phone from his pocket and turned on the flashlight app. "Are you crazy, woman? We're ten feet from ice cream, and I'm about to dare you to eat whatever concoction I make up. You wouldn't want to back down from a dare, would you?"

❉ ❉ ❉

A rush of feelings swirled through Tegan's chest as she stared at Wyatt over the glow of his phone. "No." She laughed, keeping her voice low even as she wanted to shout from the heavens. "I wouldn't want to do that."

"That's my girl." He gave her a wicked look, complete with an out-of-character eyebrow wiggle—not that she really knew his whole character, but this was a side of him she hadn't yet glimpsed. "Now close your eyes."

"It's dark."

"Back talk? Really? I'm putting pickles in your sundae."

She squeaked and pressed her lips together. "I'llbegood," she mumbled.

He just grinned as he moved away.

She leaned back against the island and closed her eyes, willing her heart to stop racing. It didn't listen.

The freezer door opened, then closed. Wyatt really moved quite stealthily. She didn't even hear him take anything out, but she did hear the quiet tink of a spoon touching ceramic.

A slight pop—a jar opening, maybe.

Then the hiss of something that she hoped to God was whipped cream.

And finally freezer again, or the fridge, she couldn't tell which, and things were put away.

He returned with her bowl behind his back. "Eyes closed."

Ooops. "I didn't mean to open them."

"Likely story."

She squeezed them shut and didn't even cheat.

He was wearing the pink t-shirt, after all, even if he had put a flannel shirt on over top. It was his turn to torture her, fair was fair.

His knees brushed hers as he sat in front of her. "Now. The dare officially is to eat at least three spoonfuls of this mystery sundae, no matter what I put in it."

She wrinkled her nose. "Okay."

"Do you have any allergies?"

"Pickles," she deadpanned.

"Rats," he said just as straight. "Hope you've got your epipen handy."

So no pickles, then. She exhaled. "No allergies. Other than pickles. And...anchovies."

He laughed. "Open up."

She wanted to. Her jaw even hinged a bit. But her lips remained firmly sealed.

Wyatt tapped the spoon against the side of the bowl. The wet scraping sound wasn't helping.

"I'm not—mmf!" She protested around the unexpected mouthful of...oh my. She rolled the familiar yet totally surprising tastes around in her mouth.

Peanut butter and jelly, or something just like that.

Definitely peanut butter. And...not jam. Maybe a fruit spread or a compote. Creamy ice cream that made her groan. Oh, yes. "More," she whispered, and he gave her another taste, this one different. Whipped cream and sugary crushed nuts, with more of that fruity sweetness along the edges of the spoon. She chased it with her tongue.

"One more to win the dare," he rumbled, and she blinked her eyes open.

"I'm eating every last bite."

He just grinned and fed her another spoonful, this one with peanut butter again, and she couldn't get over how clever it was.

"How did you…" She grabbed the spoon. This would go faster if she served herself. "I mean, the peanut butter is ribboned so nicely."

"It's in a squeeze tube up on the shelf. I just spotted it."

"Resourceful. I approve." She gobbled another two spoonfuls before remembering her manners. "Would you like some?"

He pulled another spoon from his pocket. "I wasn't sure you were going to offer."

"I almost didn't. You could give Allison a run for her job."

"Sure, if the only thing I'd need to make as pastry chef would be ice cream sundaes that appeal to the inner eight-year-old."

"Eleven." She blushed as he gave her a curious look. "That's how old my inner camper is. It's a thing in my head."

"What's so special about eleven?"

"That's how old I was when my dad remarried." Oh. She dropped her spoon, and he sat back, giving her a minute she hadn't known she needed. A hot tear tried to take up residence in the corner of her eye, but she wasn't having any of that. She cleared her throat. "That was a shitty summer. And my two weeks at camp were a refuge of sorts."

Wyatt nodded.

"I guess this is a shitty summer, too. Was, anyway. And I...this week...you know. I had high expectations and it's good, but it's bringing up some stuff, too. Whatever. Feelings." She blew a raspberry.

He just gave her another nod like raspberries were a completely acceptable way to deal with feelings. "Yeah."

She focused on the sundae. "This is really good."

"I have some skills."

"This one I'm keeping my little secret."

He gave her a slow smile as he set his spoon next to hers, then took the bowl from her hands. "Come here."

"What?"

"I want to give you another secret."

"Is it a kiss?"

He laughed. "It is."

She leaned over, and he pulled her right into his lap, so she was sitting sideways, her legs hanging over one of his thighs, her back braced against the other. He cupped her cheek and rubbed his thumb against the corner of her mouth.

"You are the brightest light I have ever seen. You are a shining star. And I'm glad you came back to camp."

"Who are you and what did you do with GI Joe?"

"He's got a soft spot for hippies," he whispered, his lips covering hers softly. It didn't stay a gentle kiss for long.

They tumbled sideways, stretching out on the kitchen floor. And they made out like teenagers until the middle of the night.

Only when Tegan rubbed her eyes did Wyatt let her go. "Bedtime," he said gruffly.

"I don't want to," she said softly.

"The kitchen staff will be in here in a few hours and they're probably going to object."

She groaned. "True story."

Wyatt grabbed the bowl and spoons and stuffed them in a bag. "I'm going to sneak it into the breakfast dishes tomorrow."

"Clever."

"Only if I succeed."

She had no doubt he would.

CHAPTER EIGHT

Tegan was pretty sure dawn crawled over the horizon ten minutes after her head hit the pillow. But that didn't stop her from waking up—all the way up, eyes wide open and brain on alert—as soon as she heard the clap of a screen door.

Without hesitation, she climbed out of bed and peeked out the back window. Wyatt was warming up, and he had some gear next to him. A gym bag, a giant log, and a cement block.

She dashed into the bathroom and combed her hair into an ever-so-casual ponytail, brushed her teeth, and then wrapped her blanket around her shoulders as she eased open the back door.

"Morning," she said as he put down the gym bag he'd just picked up. It looked and sounded like it was full of rocks, and she didn't want to imagine what he was going to do with it. "You didn't get much sleep last night."

"Neither did you." He flashed her a quick grin. "You could go back to bed. I'll be sure to come pick you up for breakfast."

Well that made her heart flutter. But she wasn't going anywhere. "I'd rather watch you do this."

He jogged over and brushed a quick kiss against the corner of her mouth that made her heart flutter.

"Be my guest," he whispered against her skin before pulling back.

She reached his hands. He'd taped them up for this workout, protecting the blisters that she'd doctored for him.

"I'm fine," he said with a wink.

So fine, she thought to herself as she kissed his palm before letting him go. She settled on the step and watched as he set his phone to be a timer.

"No laughing at me when it gets hard," he said, pointing his index finger her way.

"Scout's honour."

"Were you a Girl Scout?"

She laughed. "No. Always wanted to, but it didn't happen for various reasons." Parental reasons. First the fighting, then the divorce, and her mother being overworked and not able to handle one more thing, like remembering a scouting schedule. Or paying for extracurriculars. "But then I came to camp, and learned scouting-adjacent things. I can still start a mean fire."

His phone beeped, and he grabbed the weighted-down gym bag and threw it into the air. *Threw it*. A bag full of rocks, over his head. She gasped as he hung on to the straps, letting them stretch taut before he swung it down and across his body, past his hips.

Up and down, like a kamikaze lumberjack.

When his phone beeped, he switched sides. It was no less terrifying. She was sure the rocks would smash him in the head, but he kept the fluid rhythm with ease. On the next beep, he jumped over to the log. This was a quick stepping thing, feet on either side of it, running up and down the log, stepping up and down at the same time.

The concrete block was hefted onto his shoulder while he held his opposite arm straight up above him and did a deep squat.

That one wasn't so scary. And his ass…

This was a very good morning, indeed.

The next time through, he did everything at half the speed as the first round, and the sweat started rolling down his body. His shorts started to cling to his powerful thighs, and Tegan couldn't drag her eyes away from the flex and pulse of those muscles.

Especially now that she knew just how good all that brawn felt when pressed against her.

Before the third round, he stopped to take a short water break and slowly walked toward her as he drank from his water bottle. When he stopped in front of her, she resisted the urge to reach out and slide her fingers along his glistening, corded forearm.

Fresh, hard-working man sweat had suddenly leapt to the top of her Things That Are Definitely Hot list.

He clearly didn't mind being ogled, but petting him mid-workout might cross the line into objectifying him for his perfect form.

"This is going to sound like a stupid question, but is your job really this physically demanding?"

He nodded. "It won't be long before I'm deployed overseas. I...do a lot of unconventional things. Climbing, carrying, endurance stuff. Lives depend on it."

"Wow." Now she felt bad about keeping him from his sleep. And the reminder that he was here, now, but would very much *not* be anywhere accessible to her in the near future was an important one, too.

There was no room for soft, squishy feelings in this thing they were playing with.

"I'm gonna do that a few times more. You good to keep hanging out?"

Good? Watching him was a *treat*. "Yeah. I'm cool."

He grinned at her and she didn't feel cool in the least. She was hot and flustered and entirely too affected by this guy who was way out of her league and definitely long-term off-limits.

But he made her ice cream sundaes and let her watch him work out.

He asked about her feelings and gave her space to just ramble and talk at her own pace.

Wyatt Henderson was secretly a very nice guy.

Danger. Alert. Warning.

It didn't matter what heads-up her brain tried to send to her heart, her heart didn't care. It had already flipped for him, and all she could do now was hang on tight and try to be realistic about what could happen.

One week. Four more nights.

A bunch of sunny afternoons and snuggly evenings.

A totally made-up swim meet and as many funny dares as they could squeeze into the time they had left.

She snuggled deeper into her blanket as she watched him reset his make-shift workout center. He was breathing hard and covered in sweat, but he didn't miss a beat when his phone beeped. Even when his arms shook and the strain seemed like it might be too much, he kept swinging that bag of rocks. The log-jog, as she'd taken to calling the second exercise, was still a piece of cake for him, but the squats…

It had taken him five rounds of exercises, but Wyatt finally seemed beat. His squats were slow and he had to fight to keep his form. He dropped the concrete block in between switching from one shoulder to the other.

In general, he looked *done*.

But he kept going, slow and steady. She was beyond impressed.

"That looked really hard," she said when he finally

89

finished and came over to stretch against the back of her cabin.

"That's the point."

"You didn't want to stop?"

He laughed. "Sure, I guess." He winked. "I'd like to crawl back into bed, too. But there's gonna be lots of times when I need that strength, and stopping won't be an option. I do this now so I can do that then. I'm training my mind as much as my body."

"Oh." That made sense, and she felt a little bad. "That's impressive in more ways than one."

He shrugged. "Just doing my job."

"Thank you."

He grabbed the top of his foot and stretched the front of his leg. "I'm going to take a quick shower, but after that, you want to walk to breakfast together?"

She nodded. "I guess I should dress for the day, too."

His eyes lit up. "You're just wearing PJs under that?" She flashed him a quick look at her tank top and short shorts, and he bit his lower lip as he raked his gaze over her body.

She didn't mind being ogled, either.

"Shower time," he muttered, and she wrapped the blanket around herself again.

"Yep."

"Sneak me into your cabin and we can shower

together." He winked and stepped back.

He might be kidding, but she was tempted. "We could…"

He stopped his backwards retreat and leapt forward instead, joining her on the cabin's small back porch.

"I'm all sweaty," he said apologetically as she wound her arms around his neck.

"I don't care. Kiss me already."

This kiss was hot and claiming, instantly deep. She plastered herself against him, her blanket falling around her feet.

"I told myself I wasn't going to do this," he said against her mouth.

"God, why not?" She sucked on his lower lip. They should spend every minute left of camp making out. New plan. "Too much talking, GI Joe. Shut up and kiss me."

He laughed and did as she demanded, laying a sizzling one on her that made her toes curl. But he still pulled back again. "Are you sure this is a good idea?"

"Yes."

"Don't answer that so quickly."

She laughed. "It's all I've thought about since last night. I promise I'm not being glib about it. But life is short. Plus…I dare you."

"To do what?"

"Cut loose. Just be in the moment. Kiss me, over and over again, all week long, and don't worry about what comes next. Nothing comes next, right? So it doesn't matter."

"Tegan." He said her name like it was a complete sentence. *Tegan, be reasonable.*

She returned the volley, loading her own meaning into his name. "Wyatt." *Wyatt, be unreasonable. Be crazy. Be mine, just for a few days.*

He looked up at the brightening sky and she caught the flash of a rueful smile. "You're something else. Something amazing. What do you want with a guy like me?"

"I like you. In all your maddening ways, I like you. I want you, too," she added, lowering her voice even though they were the only two people awake at this hour. "And I don't see any good reason why we should deny ourselves." She licked her lips and teased him a little more. "Assuming you want me too, that is. Maybe I shouldn't assume."

"You can definitely assume that."

"I can?"

He looked back down at her. "Oh, yeah. And you know it."

"Then it's settled. No strings attached fun, all week long. No more thinking about what comes next."

"Okay." He lifted her off the deck and kissed her

again, then pressed her back against the door and stroked her cheek as he stared down at her. "But I'm going to shower in my own cabin. If your roommates interrupted us, that would be awkward."

"Stick in the mud," she whispered.

"First time we're naked together, I want to know we're not going to be interrupted."

"Oh…" she inhaled a shuddering breath. "Okay. Good plan."

"Soon." He lifted her hand and kissed her knuckles. "We'll figure something out."

How on earth was she supposed to make it through breakfast, never mind the rest of the day, with that promise ringing in her ears?

He reached past her and opened the door, clearly waiting for her to leave their private moment first.

"I'm going to hold you to that alone time promise," she said archly, but her wide grin betrayed how she really felt.

He just kissed her again.

Oh man, was she in trouble. The best kind.

Thirty minutes later, she exited the cabin again, this time in denim cut-offs and a tank top that made her boobs look fantastic, and practically tripped over Wyatt, who was sitting on the front porch.

"Well, hello there," he said with a wink.

She could feel her friends staring at her back with

intense curiosity. Taking a deep breath, she reached out her hand and he stood, weaving his fingers through hers.

"Hello," she whispered back, and they set off down the trail, leaving what she could only imagine was quite a stunned pair of gawkers in their wake.

Or maybe not.

Prina had called it already. Tegan totally had a camp crush on Wyatt, and it was reciprocal. That she'd tried to deny it had been foolish, and they'd surely seen right through her.

That they kept silent through breakfast was proof they were the best of friends. Nothing was said about the fact Tegan couldn't stop looking at Wyatt and smiling at him—and he was grinning right back.

Of course, her friends weren't the only ones at the table. And Grady and Danny were all over *their* friend as soon as breakfast was over and Wyatt glanced at her and asked, "What do you want to do today?"

"What does that mean?" Grady asked, a wicked grin spreading across his face.

"Yeah." Danny waggled his eyebrows at Tegan, earning himself a heavy thud against his shoulder, courtesy of Wyatt's fist. "What? I'm just curious if you've found a fishing partner."

Tegan's cheeks heated up. "Uhh…"

Wyatt curled his hand around her hip and pulled

her close. Even better than a friendly hip bump or a secret look. "I could take you fishing. But we should probably do some swimming with the rest of your team, right?"

"You don't mind?"

"You in a swimsuit?" He glared at his friend, who'd been about to say something. "Shut up, Danny. Yeah, I don't mind. Let's get our swim on. We only have three days until we need to compete for glory, right?"

So that's what they did, for most of the morning.

Then Wyatt disappeared while she got changed for lunch, and reappeared with a basket covered in a folded blanket. He'd apparently sweet-talked Meg in the kitchen to putting together a picnic for them, and they headed up the path behind the cabins.

"You could bring your fishing gear," she offered as they headed past Cabin Nine.

"Nah," he said, taking her hand in his. "This is all I want to do this afternoon. I feel like we've done a lot of talking the last couple days, but it's all been on the surface. I want to lie in the sun and find out some Tegan secrets."

She giggled. "That's pretty…crunchy. I like it."

"I have a serious side."

"I have no doubt."

So that's what they did. Ate lunch slowly, tossing random questions back and forth.

She started. "Can I ask more about your military service?"

"Sure."

"You're...not a regular soldier, are you?"

He shook his head. "I'm special operations. Navy, not army. I'm based in Coronado."

"You're a SEAL."

"Yeah."

"And Grady and Danny, too?"

"Yep." He took a deep breath. "Sometimes we take other assignments, for career progression. That's what I was doing before I met them here."

"Ah." She wrinkled her nose. "Working in an office sucks, doesn't it? I mean, I assume it was something like that."

He grinned. "Yeah. Something like that. Office with uniforms. And a lot of politics."

"Gross."

"No kidding." He handed over a box of chopped veggies. "How about you? No more insurance company. Wait, sorry. You didn't want to talk about that."

"It's fine. I'm not grumpy with you anymore." She shrugged. "Yeah, no more of that. I don't know what I'm going to do next. It's not like I have a passion for corporate communications or anything."

"What do you have a passion for?"

"S'mores." It was a cheeky answer. "And the outdoors. I love stuff like this, but I don't know if I want that much of a nomad life, you know? Summer job at a camp or a resort, winter job...I don't know." But she did. A sudden pang of longing surged through her chest.

"What?"

She wrinkled her nose. "Nothing."

He tug through the picnic basket and lifted two cupcakes out from the bottom. "Can I tempt you with a truth cupcake?"

"That's not a thing."

He winked. "How about I take my shirt off and let you eat it off my chest?"

She howled with laughter. "That's the vainest offer I've ever received. Oh, man." She wiped her eyes, then made a circling gesture with her hand. "But yes, I'd like that very much. Off with your shirt."

CHAPTER NINE

As Wyatt peeled off his shirt, he almost lost sight of what triggered it. His skin pulled taut under Tegan's gaze, hot and achy for her touch — and he'd get it. But he wanted something else, too.

Whatever had put that look on her face. He wanted that secret. He wanted to know things about her that others didn't. He wanted, as selfish as it was, to be her lover and her confidant.

Camp was most certainly fucking with his head.

He didn't care about intimacies. About shared secrets and whispered stories. He most certainly never cared about what saddened a fuck buddy. Fucking was a fun release, a stress reducer and an escape from thinking too hard about anything for an hour or two.

Of course, if he'd thought of Tegan as a potential fuck buddy, he'd have taken her in the kitchen the night before.

Or on the back porch of her cabin this morning.

Tested out that shower invite, and not really cared about who'd seen or heard them, or whether or not they got interrupted by protesting roommates.

She's different. It was a cliche, and he knew it. Yeah, she was different. She wasn't just a beautiful woman he wanted to bang. He had a crush on her. A big one. The kind of crush that could go somewhere if he were another man, with another life, maybe that made the feelings even bigger.

Bigger and bittersweet. That was it. His feelings for her had been bittersweet from the start, and in hindsight, maybe there'd been a reason for that—maybe he'd been attracted to her from the second she'd picked up his rucksack.

Maybe he'd known as soon as he'd heard her voice that he'd want more of her than he could rightly ask for.

Secrets, for one thing.

Love, for another.

Whoa. Nobody was allowed to think the L-word.

Luckily Tegan couldn't see the mess of feelings in his head. She sank her teeth lightly into the skin on his abs. "Give me that cupcake or I'm just going to eat you for dessert," she whispered as she licked him.

"Promise?" He groaned as she moved up his torso. "Do that again. Wait, no. Cupcake."

She laughed as he set the cupcake on his sternum. "So I just…eat it?"

"No hands. And for each bite, you need to tell me something good. Start with what you really want to do this winter."

She wrinkled her nose. "That's just a pipe dream."

"Spill."

"This better be a good cupcake." She shifted on top

of him, and he forced his cock not to swell in response. He was already thick, half-hard just from her nearness, and—too late. "Or that's another option," she said, sighing huskily as she rolled more deliberately against his shameless erection.

"Fine," he growled, grabbing the cupcake with one hand and flipping her onto her back with the other arm. "We'll do this the mean way."

"What's the mean way?" she asked, her eyes bright as he swiped the cupcake against her bottom lip, leaving a trail of icing behind.

He licked it off, but pulled back as she chased his tongue with her own.

"Oh," she breathed. "So mean."

"You should take off your top, too." He reared up, resting on his heels as she wriggled beneath him. As soon as she'd tossed her tank top aside, revealing a bra that wasn't technically more skimpy than the bikinis he'd already seen. It still made him light-headed. He dropped again, caging her in with one hand up by her shoulder and his knees pressing her thighs wide open to limit her mobility. "I've got you now."

Her eyes went wide. "No," she said, feigning fear. "Whatever will I do?"

He danced the cupcake past her mouth again and she parted her lips, her eyelids fluttering shut. Damn, but that was a pretty sight.

100

"Want another taste?"

"I didn't get the first one, you stole it," she whispered.

He brushed the icing against her lip again, and watched her lick it off. An unholy groan shuddered from deep inside him. "Tell me your secret, Tegan."

"Why?"

"Because I want to lick this icing off every inch of your body, but I can't do it until I know what you want more than anything else in the world."

Her eyelids blinked open. "I want to be a ski instructor." Her eyes flared in surprise. "How do you do that?"

"Do what?" He touched the cupcake to her shoulder, then dipped his head to lick her skin clean.

"Ask me questions that I don't even know the answers to myself."

"But you do, clearly."

"I didn't…" She gave him a rueful grin. "Okay. I knew that. But I didn't think I could say it out loud."

"And then you did. That's cool. Especially skiing. That's badass."

"Do you ski?"

He shook his head. "Cross-country, sure. But not downhill. Never been." Another rich kid activity that Wisconsin farm boys didn't get, but he wasn't going to point that out. "Moved to California when I was eighteen. I can surf. Maybe snowboarding might be similar."

"No Arctic training?" she teased.

"Not that kind, anyway."

"I could teach you."

With a start, he realized he keenly wanted that to happen. But by the time the snow fell anywhere near here, or anywhere near California for that matter, he'd be on the other side of the world, fighting the good fight.

And he keenly wanted that, too. He always had, and always would.

"Maybe one day," he rumbled, his voice suddenly catching, and he moved down her body, swirling icing down her midsection like a slalom slope. He flattened his tongue against the softness of her belly, and swept back up the same path, tossing the cupcake aside when he was finally at her mouth again.

"What about my turn?" she asked breathlessly.

"There's another cupcake in the basket." He cupped the back of her neck and swept his tongue inside her mouth, exploring and cajoling until she was kissing back as hard as he needed—hard enough to push out the longing for skiing lessons and hot chocolate in front of a roaring fire.

He sank into her, skin to skin from the waist up, and rubbed his free hand up her side, over her curves and around the edges of her bra. "Is this okay?"

She nodded jerkily and he stroked his fingertips along the edge of the cup, finding another slice of skin he hadn't yet worshiped. Trailing his mouth down her neck, he worked his way there, and kissed the paler skin as he exposed it. She was breathing hard, her breasts rising toward him with each inhale, when her nipple popped into view.

Hot, pulsing desire thudded through him at the sight of that hidden bit of her. Pink and tight, already hard, the peak made his mouth water. He breathed her name against her body as he engulfed it with his lips, trying to be gentle, but probably failing.

He was a dying, hungry man. Restraint was an abstract thought that faded even further when Tegan's hands slid into his hair, urging him closer.

He stroked her other breast, coaxing the other bra cup down until both breasts were free and plumped together. Then he went back and forth, gorging himself on the sweetness of her skin. He felt her hands on him, felt when she released her grip on his hair and moved her fingers over his shoulders and down his arms, but when she hit his waistband, it was still a surprise.

"Is this okay?" she asked, echoing his question, and he groaned against her chest. Fuck, they both needed to be naked.

He needed to be inside her more than he needed his next breath.

Before she could shove his shorts too far, he grabbed the condom he'd had the foresight to bring, then rolled onto his back so he could watch her shimmy out of those cutoff shorts.

The condom went to the side of the blanket, because he had other things to do first. Like kiss her calf. Her knee. Her thigh, which started to shake as she fumbled with stripping off her underwear.

"Ticklish?" he asked, his voice rougher than sandpaper as he got his first look of her entirely naked. He pressed his fingertips more firmly against the warmth of her leg.

Backlit by the sun, she was a bronze goddess. When she moved closer, blocking the light, he got a tantalizing glimpse of pale tan lines and neat, dark curls between her legs before his hands were moving of their own volition, cupping her bottom and hauling her close. She laughed as she sprawled on top of him, a husky, sexy sound that went straight to his lizard brain and activated his inner caveman.

"Not particularly," she said, scraping her teeth against his lower lip. "Just…no teasing. But please touch me." She paused and blinked down at him, her face flushed and gorgeous. "Take me, if you want."

Oh, fuck. He wanted. He flipped them again and

104

kept his gaze locked on hers as he memorized the feel of her body against his palms, the curve and dip and rise of her flesh before he found her wet and ready for him.

She rolled her hips, encouraging his touch to quest a little deeper, and he stroked lower, circling her entrance before pulling some of that heady slickness up to her clit.

Her eyes hooded as he figured out what she liked. A little roll, a good amount of pressure. A swipe of his fingers through her folds made her shiver and when he fit just the tip of his middle finger against her, she bucked her hips and welcome him inside her.

She reached for him, too. Her touch was deft, surer than his was, and it didn't take long before they had a quiet, erotic rhythm figured out. Their arms brushed as they stroked each other, electricity sparking against his skin there and everywhere else she touched him.

He added another finger, stretching her open, and she shifted beneath him.

The first wet brush of his cock against her sex scrambled his brain cells. *Yes, take her, now, do it.* He shuddered and jerked his hips, lifting his cock more firmly into her grip.

His hand was in the way. He couldn't just fuck into her. But oh God, he wanted to. And when she let go, twisting to reach for the condom, he knew his slick plan of getting her off first was out the window.

When it came to Tegan, he was officially un-slick. Zero plan.

All feelings and fumbling and hoping for the best.

She sheathed him as he braced himself above her, then she spread her legs wide and notched them together.

He watched, unable to breath, as his cock disappeared into her body. The feeling as he pressed into her was indescribable, but he forced himself to think of it, actively. To record it forever. "Tegan," he growled, and she cupped his cheek.

"More," she breathed.

He was on the edge. He needed to ride the wave of *holyshitthiswoman* that was surging through him before he gave her more. But he jerked his heavy, unfocused attention back to her face and kissed her as he pressed into her.

He could give her that. He could worship her and love her as she undid him in the simplest of ways.

"Wyatt," she keened, her grip tightening on his hips. "Oh, yes, there."

He flexed inside her. "That good?"

"Yes…" She rolled her head back and moaned, totally uninhibited.

Again. I want to hear that again.

106

He hadn't see this coming. He was tumbling hard and fast toward feelings he didn't want to name.

With a growl, he snapped his hips back, then thrust deep again, his need to hear her pleasure finally overriding his own shaky lock on his own release.

Her legs rocked up his body as he surged into her. He found her hands and tangled their fingers together, pressing hard against the blanket. Leverage so he could wring the most gorgeous cries from her sweet mouth.

And maybe he was holding her down so he could pretend he was in control.

She arched beneath him and he ducked his head to suck her nipple into his mouth again. When her thighs start trembling, and her moans grew shaky, too, he let himself go, and maybe there'd been some control there after all.

Because it was all gone now, and he was a raging, seething beast above her, holding her against him as he brought them together, deep and fast and furious. She was slick and he was hard. It was perfect. Dirty.

Hot.

Perfect. The word echoed through his mind, then morphed. Perfect. Perfect Tegan.

Tegan. *Tegan.* As he thought her name on a stuttering auto-repeat, his hips jerking faster and faster, she gripped him with her thighs and her pussy and her heart. And then when he thought he just might die, she shattered beneath him, falling slack in his arms, and he fell on top of her, his legs shoving hers wide. His hips pistoning still as his balls pulled tight, he let out a shout that would probably be heard all the way back at camp.

And as the aftershocks rippled through him and he tumbled to his side, Tegan curling up against him, all he he could think was, *again.*

CHAPTER TEN

"So, cupcakes do it for you?" Tegan grinned as Wyatt growled, then fell back against the blanket.

She was going to be so sore tomorrow.

She blushed.

And he was a *cuddler*. That made her hot and flushed in an entirely different way, because she hadn't seen that coming. But every time she shifted away, he followed. One of his hands stroked up and down her spine, tangling with her hair at the top and patting her butt at the bottom. It was the kind of possessive touching she'd always wanted from her boyfriends and never gotten.

Wyatt would be the kind of guy to pull a girl into his lap, just to hold her.

They dressed, slowly, but then tumbled again to the blanket. This time they lay facing each other. Tegan traced Wyatt's jaw, now well peppered with stubble. "You have to shave all the time, don't you?"

He twisted his head and kissed her fingertips. "When I'm on base. Not when I'm operational. I'm the crazy guy with the beard and sunglasses you sometimes see on the news. Of course, not really me, but—"

"I get it." She didn't want to think about him

disguising his features because of where he was going or what he'd be doing. She didn't want to think about his life being in danger, no matter how capable she was sure he would be.

"You don't mind the stubble?"

"Mind it?" She touched her fingertips to her chest where her skin was pink from the rub of his face. "No. I love it."

"Even if I gave you beard burn somewhere else?" His eyes burned as he leaned in, until his lips brushed against hers. "The inside of your thighs, maybe?"

"Yes. Do that." She closed her eyes as he pressed her lips open softly, his tongue teasing against hers.

And then he did that, and it was was glorious.

They headed back in time for cocktail hour, mostly because the remaining cupcake wasn't really enough to refuel them after their afternoon energy expenditure, and also because they hoped to avoid ribbing from their friends for missing the rest of the day.

They were successful on the former goal, because the staff had laid out a yummy trail mix and pretzel bar to go along with the pre-dinner drinks, but avoiding being made fun of? Epic fail on that front.

Of course, they did arrive at cocktail hour holding hands. And maybe stupid grins.

Plus there was that beard burn, although Tegan had stopped at the cabin to put on yoga pants and a higher-neck t-shirt to cover it up. But she was probably wearing the emotional equivalent of a neon sign. **This Girl Just Got Banged But Good. By THAT Guy.**

"You guys disappeared," Grady said with a smirk.

Wyatt stayed silent. That didn't stop them.

"Now we can all pair off for real. Boy girl, boy girl, boy girl." Danny winked at Molly. "We can even organize sleepovers."

Tegan bit her lip, trying not to laugh as her friend rolled her eyes. "The only way you're going to see me in my PJs is if you do a cabin raid."

"Who said anything about PJs? I sleep in the buff."

"Really?" Molly lowered her voice. "So if I were to short-sheet your bed, and fill it with spiders, you'd come running out buck naked?"

"And leap right in your bed, baby girl."

"How unfortunate." Molly stuck out her tongue and ducked as Danny lazily reached for her.

Prina strolled over with a couple of women from Cabin Two, clearly a diversion tactic that worked, and she gave Tegan a look that said, *you owe me*.

Without a doubt.

"You wanna go and sit on the dock for a while?" Wyatt murmured against her ear.

Yes, yes she did. She nodded and they left the

cocktail hour as quickly as they'd arrived at it, nabbing snacks and a glass of hard lemonade for her and a beer for him on their way out of the lodge and across the green lawn toward the lake.

"My friends can be dicks."

"My friends can handle them."

He snorted. "That sounds dirty."

"Kind of meant it to…but I probably shouldn't tease."

He gave a low, pained chuckle. "I haven't worn you out yet today?"

She shrugged. He probably had, but that didn't mean she didn't still *want* more.

He wrapped his arm around her waist and kissed her neck. "Best afternoon of my life. I'm going to remember the way your ass looked in those shorts for a long time."

Ouch. Nothing killed a lady boner like an accidental reminder that it wouldn't be long before they were just memories for each other. But she'd staked those boundaries first—for her own good—and the gentle squeeze on her hip followed by a caress across her back, up to her neck where he rested his hand, wiped away that momentary annoyance.

It was what it was. Nothing to be done about that. They lived on opposite coasts. *You were already thinking about leaving New York.* Yeah, but for some place like…

Baltimore or Philly. Somewhere on an Amtrak line that still got her to Broadway plays and holiday shopping on Fifth Avenue. Somewhere driving distance to her mother.

And one didn't start to think about moving across the country just because one got one's world rocked in an afternoon.

That was the definition of creepy.

"Penny for your thoughts."

She jerked her attention up to Wyatt, who was watching her intently. "You sound like my grandmother."

"Mine, too, I guess."

"Are your grandparents still…"

He shook his head. "All passed on. I never knew my dad's dad, he died when my father was a teenager. I have vague memories of the other three, but they were all gone by the time I was in middle school."

"I'm sorry."

He reached out and brushed a lock of hair off her cheek. "Serious talk. Everything okay?"

"I was thinking about my mother. She's getting older and I'm…" She paused and considered her word choice. "Molly and I have talked about moving. Well, I want to leave the city, and she's flexible. She can work anywhere. We talked about Atlanta, but that's really too far from my mom. That's what I was thinking

113

about."

Sort of.

"Being here makes you think about adventures elsewhere?"

In a manner of speaking. "Yeah."

"You ever ask your mother what she thinks?"

"You don't understand the guilt trips she can pull." Tegan laughed. "And she doesn't even know she's doing it."

Wyatt leaned over and set his beer on the edge of the dock, then sat down carefully, his legs dangling just above the water. He reached his arm out wide. "Come here."

She nestled against him and took a slow sip of her drink.

He fed her a cashew from the trail mix.

Something sweet and soft unfurled in her chest, and she closed her eyes.

"I know a little something about family obligations," he said slowly, stretching his words out. "And every family is different. Some are totally dysfunctional. Others are rough, but there's love there, deep down. That's probably where my family sits. I'd like to say when I told them that I was joining the Navy that it went well."

She peered up at him. "It didn't?"

He grimaced. "Not at all. There was yelling. Harsh

reminders about my duty to take over the farm."

"But you did it anyway."

"It was my calling." He shrugged. "And if my parents couldn't see that, then I was okay with them being mad at me."

"Wow." She was so not okay with her parents being mad at her. Or anyone else, for that matter. Except Wyatt… She giggled.

"What?"

"I was just thinking that you're the first person I've ever purposely pissed off."

"An honor," he said dryly.

"I think it is," she sighed. "I'm just not one hundred percent sure how. But there's something nice there."

"More trail mix?"

She accepted his offering, but it was hardly taking the edge off. "I'm starving."

"Dinner should be soon. Although that'll be less fun for you than for me, since you'll be having some variation on twigs and leaves."

"Seriously, you're pulling the Vegan Girl thing back into play?" But it gave her a little thrill, and most definitely made mincemeat of her melancholy. She swivelled around, sitting cross-legged as she glared at him. "So uncool."

He grinned and popped a dried cranberry in his mouth. "Uh huh. What are you going to do about it, beat me up?"

"Haha, very funny. Me and my puny tofu-fueled arms, right? Joke's on you, buster. I can bench a mean…I don't know, what's a good weight to bench?"

He leaned in and kissed her nose. "You're perfect just the way you are."

"I could take you."

"I bet you could. Do you just want to demolish a steak right now?"

"No." She regretted telling him she wasn't really a vegetarian.

"Come on."

She groaned. "Maybe a little."

"I can sneak you one."

"That's the sweetest thing anyone's ever said to me."

"Really?"

She giggled. "Maybe. Really, I appreciate the thought. I'll stick to the delicious food I've ordered, though. It's all good."

He set down the trail mix and cupped her face in his hands. "You're a good friend."

"Friendship is everything."

He nodded as he leaned in. "It is."

Her breath hitched as his lips grazed hers. "You're a good friend, too."

"I try." He exhaled, his breath warm and soft

116

against her mouth.

She melted. "Mmm. You succeed."

"Do all your friends kiss you like this?" Another brush of his lips, this one sending tingles down her spine. No, she'd never had anyone give her tingles the way he did.

"Maybe."

"I'll have to try harder, then."

"Try harder for what?"

"Top spot on the kissing friends list."

Oh, Wyatt. You already have that locked.

❀ ❀ ❀

He couldn't stop touching her.

This might be what people meant when they talked about floating on cloud nine. How many times had he rolled his eyes hard at that expression, and any others like it?

And now he was sporting what he was sure was a dopey-as-hell grin.

Through dinner and the bonfire, they bumped legs and brushed fingers. He even pulled her into his lap as the night wore on, because he wanted her there.

She didn't seem to mind.

When it was time to head to the cabins, he held her hand and tugged her back a bit from the crowd. His chest was so full he thought it might burst, and somehow he wanted to find a way to tell her that.

But as their friends pulled ahead, taking the soundtrack of laughter and chatter with them, he found himself mute.

Four days. It was nothing in the grand scheme of things. And yeah, he'd seen lives changed irrevocably in a lot less time than that, but big feelings?

He couldn't trust himself in this territory. It was foreign and he was woefully ill-equipped to translate whatever was happening into words that made sense.

His body knew what to do, though. Knew to draw her around so they were facing each other, their bodies close enough to feel where her softness started to give to his harder bulk. Her breasts against his chest, his cock against her belly.

"I don't want to say goodnight," he murmured, caressing her cheek.

She pressed her face into his hand. "I know."

He curved over her, breathing in the lingering smoke on her hair and the marshmallow sweetness on her breath.

But when he kissed her, a ruthless, sudden capture of her mouth, nothing masked the taste of her. And even with his hard, brutal pace, she fell immediately into his rhythm, pushing and pulling as they poured everything into the kiss because it was all they had tonight.

He squeezed her waist, then slid his hands up her ribcage. Lifting her a hair off the ground, and right into his body. He didn't want anything, not even air, to separate them.

She clung to him.

It was a shared mission now. Closeness. Clinging to the magic—yes, fucking magic—of the day, because what if they woke up and it turned out to be a dream?

He didn't care if that was sappy.

His hands started roaming. The edge of her breast. Down her back to cup her ass. The sweet overflow of her flesh made his blood pound in his veins, until a dull roar filled his ears.

It better not be a dream. He wasn't done with her. Not by a long shot.

They slid apart, then crashed together again. Her lips tugged at his, then parted, slick and swollen. The wet warmth made him think of her pussy, and God, he wanted to spin her around and take her against a tree.

Tomorrow, maybe.

The thought of another day of adventurous sex filled him with a rush of pleasure. "I want to take you fishing tomorrow," he whispered. "Another picnic."

"Another picnic blanket?" She smiled, a quick flash in the dark. "I can't wait."

He tangled his hand in her hair and dropped his

forehead to rest against hers. "I'll think of you all night."

"I should hope so," she teased, her breath hot and puffy against his mouth.

"I'm going to walk you to your cabin now, and kiss you goodnight."

"In a minute," she whispered before licking her way back into his mouth.

It took a lot longer than a minute. And once he'd finally watched her disappear inside, he sat on his own porch for a long time and stared up at the stars.

CHAPTER ELEVEN

A steady drizzle of rain plinking on the cabin's roof woke Tegan on Tuesday morning. She blinked her eyes open to a dreary gray morning, then closed them again.

Surely Wyatt wouldn't be working out in the rain. She could go back to sleep for a bit.

You sure about that? She rolled to the side, casting about for any little sound that would signify he was outside. Finally her curiosity won out and she climbed out of bed. Maybe by the end of the week she'd be trained to be a hardcore morning person.

The space between their cabins was empty.

She stood still at the window, surprised at the depth of her disappointment. Not that she wanted him to be suffering in the rain. She just wanted him. In front of her, inspiring her...

She looked across to his porch. Maybe she should get dressed and head over there. Wake him up.

As if she'd summoned him, his cabin door opened, but it wasn't Wyatt that stepped out. Danny moved onto the porch, still yawning. He was wearing running gear.

So they were all insane.

He swung his arms wide, then moved them in circles. Forward and backward. He warmed up his legs in the same way, then paused when the door opened again.

It was Grady this time. They shared a brief conversation, then Danny jumped off the porch and headed out at a run. Grady scowled and pulled his hoody up over his head before following down the path at a brisk pace—not running. More like hunting coffee.

Which meant Wyatt was alone.

She grinned and sprinted back to her bed. She dumped her blanket on the mattress. Then she pulled on her rain jacket and slipped on her sandals before quietly ducking out the back door.

She eased her way into the boys' cabin and shook off her raincoat. Wyatt was fast asleep, flat on his back, his light blanket shoved low on his body. He slept in shorts, nothing else, and his chest looked particularly broad in the small twin bed. He was like a giant, muscle-bound teddy bear. Perfect for snuggling up with.

Or…

She tiptoed over and climbed onto his bed, resting between his legs.

"Wyatt," she breathed. "Good morning."

He half-groaned, half-smiled. Then he snored.

She laughed quietly to herself and leaned over, planting her hands on either side of his hips. She kissed the warm skin of his abs. He was so gentle at rest. Such a counter to the rough tightness of his body while awake. She loved the restless energy he'd poured into making love to her the day before, but having him at her mercy like this, hers to explore and taste and touch—this was an unexpected thrill.

She breathed in the clean, sweet scent of his skin, and it made her mouth water. She followed the trail of crisp hair that disappeared under his waistband and kissed his semi-hard cock through the soft fabric.

A slow, thick pulse against her face was reward and encouragement rolled into one. She rubbed her nose up the growing length of him, then covered his erection with one hand as she snuck her fingers of the other under the elastic waistband.

"Whadya think you're doing?" Wyatt mumbled, his big hands closing over her wrists.

"Morning blow job," she whispered back.

"Tegan." He exhaled roughly and loosened his grip on her.

"Your roommates are gone. Danny went running, Grady looked like he was heading in search of an breakfast."

He nodded, and she took the opportunity to pull his cock out of his shorts. He'd felt incredible inside her, and her belly clenched at the memory of how good that had been. But now, seeing him up close, she felt differently again about him. More...powerful, especially as his body reacted swiftly to her touch.

"Whoa." His hands fluttered next to her head and she grinned up at him.

"How much time do you think we have?"

He shoved himself up onto one elbow and scrubbed his other hand over his face as she resumed her mission to get him in her mouth.

"I don't give a fuck. Let's barricade the door and never let them back in." He groaned and tipped his head back as she slid her tongue around his crown. "Uhh... probably an hour? Danny will run at least that long. Grady isn't likely to head back through the rain any time soon. Oh, God. Yes. Do that with your tongue."

He bucked up into her mouth and she swallowed him down to her fist.

He stopped talking then, but between the adorable grunts and the restless shifting of his hips, she knew she was on the right track.

Giving head was usually a means to an end. A tit-for-tat bit of foreplay that didn't fail to impress a guy. But she rarely enjoyed it like she was now.

She was enjoying the heck out of this one. And it was making her hot, too. That was unexpected.

Pressing her thighs together, she exaggerated her back arch, pressing her hips into the air so Wyatt could see her ass behind her head. *I'm yours, all yours*, she thought, stretching like a cat.

Under his breath, he started muttering. Dirty things that made her blush and ache, made her wet — between her legs, and in her mouth, too. Like there was a hotwire connection, and each electric promise of what he wanted to do to her, wanted her to do to him, literally made her salivate for more of his taste.

And she got it. The heady scent of him filled her nose as his arousal slide over her tongue and down her throat. She pulled off and lapped against the slit at the top of his rock-hard erection. He tasted amazing, earthy and salty and good. Manly, but uniquely Wyatt.

She didn't swallow him again until he begged, and when she pulled up with her lips, a vacuum for him, he groaned a warning that he was close.

Good.

She wanted everything he might give her.

With a shout, he exploded, his release coating her tongue. She swallowed twice in quick succession, then eased off, letting the last dribble fill her hand as she stroked up his still firm length.

Without a word, he handed her a t-shirt he must have pulled off in the night.

Then he gave her a lopsided grin that made her ovaries explode.

This man. She gave him a wide-eyed look in

return, suddenly overwhelmed by him. He was too much. Too good-looking, too secretly kind, too funny, and too damn appreciative of a simple blow job.

"You, uh, didn't work out today," she said inanely.

"It was a rest day."

"Lucky me."

"No, I think the luck was all mine this morning." He tugged her up his body and rolled her beneath him. "At least so far."

"What are you doing?"

He kissed her neck, his stubble scratching her in a way that lit fire to her nerve endings and made her panties dissolve. "I was thinking first you come on my tongue. Then if you're very good you can have the D."

"The D???" she howled as he started to kiss his way down her body.

"You're wearing too many clothes."

"It didn't occur to me to streak over here naked, although from someone who refers to his junk as 'the D', maybe that's a reasonable expectation."

"Hell no. I don't want anyone else to see you naked. But strip before you climb into my bed next time." He shoved her sleep shorts down her legs and she helped him kick them away even as she kept up the argument.

"Wow. Crude and full of bossy orders. I don't know—oh." Her protest got lost in the middle of sudden, delicious pleasure as he spread her legs and dove in, licking her all over.

"I'm sorry, were you saying something about how crude I am while I was trying get to your sweet, sweet pussy?" he asked with a wink as he popped his head back up.

She shoved him back to where he belonged.

Jerk.

He'd done this yesterday, but today it was different. One night sleeping apart and everything was different, it seemed. Maybe because it wasn't their first time, it wasn't so desperate and hurried, but beneath that, there was so much affection in his touch.

Like their bond was growing exponentially with each passing minute.

He kissed her clit, a little peck right where she was most sensitive, and when her hips jumped, he softly swirled his tongue around the now-on-guard flesh. Oh, heavens.

"Yes," she begged nonsensically, so of course he backed off. She could practically feel him smiling against her sex as he went back to his lazy, licking exploration.

Her face flamed as he loved every last inch of her, only returning to her clit once she was shaking and ready to explode.

This time his tongue was firm, like a finger tip, and

he rolled it around and around until she wanted to beg him to suck instead, but words were beyond her. He'd started something insane, something shaky and magical and scary, too, deep inside her. Her eyes closed and her lips parted in a silent prayer, *more more more*, that he still somehow answered.

He clamped down on her thighs at the same moment he closed his mouth around her clit, which is the only thing that saved him from being decapitated as he launched her through the roof into the orgasm of the century.

Wrecked. That was the only word that could possible approach describing how she felt. But like a mountainside blazed by a wildfire, it didn't take long for things to come back to life.

Twitchy nerve endings, for example.

Or her desire for more Wyatt, even if she wasn't sure her body could handle it.

"Come here," she pleaded. "Kiss me."

He crawled back up her body, bringing his blanket with him. He wrapped her in his arms, tucking the soft cotton around them like a cocoon. "Good morning again."

"Wow. You could say that." She grinned against the smoothness of his skin. "And we still have time to get in the early line for breakfast."

"It's still raining." He kissed her hair. "We could

just stay here."

"But I might be hungry…"

He laughed. "Okay. We can run through the rain."

"The way I feel right now, we could dance through it." She stretched her legs down his, rubbing her smooth skin against his lightly-dusted-in-yummy-hair. She was officially hard-core in lust with this guy if she found his hairy legs hot.

"Dance in the rain?" He groaned. "You're such a…"

She poked him in the chest. "Don't say hippie."

"Optimist," he said innocently.

She snorted and cuddled deeper into his side. "You could use a little dancing in the rain. In fact…I dare you."

"That's not much of a dare."

"Do it with a smile." She rolled on top of him and winked. "I'm sure that'll be a challenge."

He barked a laugh, but it did turn into a smile then. That only lasted as long as she was on top of him, though. When she climbed off, intent now on getting him out into the rain, he reached for her. "Come here."

"Dance in the rain first. With a smile on the whole time."

"I smile."

"Rarely."

"I smile for you."

129

That was true. Warmth bloomed in her chest.

❈ ❈ ❈

She wanted him to dance in the rain? As far as dares went, it wasn't that hard. Hell, doing anything for her wasn't that big a deal. And it would officially even out their dare score, although he wasn't keeping track with the same animosity he started that first night.

But that still didn't make it easy for him. For one thing...he didn't dance. Like, genuinely, other than grinding in a club—which happened rarely and required copious amounts of booze—when was the last time he'd danced?

And also...it wasn't dancing she wanted. It wasn't the dare by itself.

She wanted to see him happy.

And he was—unexpectedly, ridiculously, kind of terrifyingly-because-it-could-end-any second happy. *Because of her.*

And now that fact was slamming him in the face like a sucker punch he hadn't seen coming, and he could feel the words bubbling up inside him.

Tegan, I know it's only been a few days, but...

He coughed and shook his head. Shit, he was shaking.

130

"Wyatt?"

"Yeah." He blinked at her and huffed out a breath. "You've got a rain coat?"

She held it up, then put it on.

He grabbed his own jacket and handed it to her along with a t-shirt he'd put on once they got to the main lodge. "You want me to dance, huh?"

"With a smile on your face."

He crowded against her, one hand sliding around her hip, the other cupping her jaw. "Then give me something to smile about, woman."

She pressed her lips against his, warm and sweet, and his heart hammered hard against his ribcage.

Let her think it was about a kiss. The filthy blow job she'd woken him up with and the gentle teasing she loved to push at him.

He'd bury the truth deep down, because there was no good way to tell a woman you loved her after two days of fighting, two days of fucking, and a non-stop reiteration that there was zero future for any kind of relationship.

He loved her, all right.

And in a few short days, he'd leave her and never look back.

CHAPTER TWELVE

The rain lifted by mid-morning, so Wyatt popped down to the kitchen and sweet-talked another picnic basket out of the chef.

This time he asked for extra cupcakes.

But it wasn't just about sex. This time they brought his fishing gear and they did that first. Tegan was a natural, and before long she was doing it all herself, which meant he got to drink a beer and cuddle her.

He was in a world of fucking trouble over this woman.

He even tried to find the first few words to start a conversation about it—*hey, so this fall...* Except he didn't know what he was doing in a few weeks. Given his last team assignment, and what Grady and Danny had given him the heads up on, it was likely he'd been headed overseas quite soon.

And *hey, so in nine months, maybe a year, I have no idea...* didn't have a very romantic ring to it.

Wanna be Facebook friends was so weak-ass he couldn't bring himself to even ask that.

Once she'd done a few catch-and-releases, they cleaned up and set the fishing stuff aside.

Tegan stood on the edge of the blanket and gave him a bashful smile.

"What?"

"Wanna get naked?"

Boom went his heart. He nodded. "So fucking much."

This time they made love slowly—the first time. He was on top at first. He sank into her by the smallest of increments, absorbing the look on her face and the feel of her body as he filled her up. Then she pushed him onto his back and rode him. He stroked her thighs and cupped her breasts. Pulled her down so they could kiss, then pushed her back up so he could watch her jiggle and bounce.

When he came deep inside her, he held himself there and pretended it meant something a hell of a lot more than a good time by the lake.

The second condom tore when they moved from a sideways position back to missionary, but they were both so damn close he just rutted against her, and she came first, rubbing her clit against the underside of his cock. Then he spilled his come on her stomach and he fucking loved that so much, he wrote his name in it.

She watched as he did it, and when he finished, she pulled his fingertip to her mouth and sucked it clean. Her eyes burned the entire time.

I love you. It was right there, but it was silenced by the even louder, *but that's crazy, right?*

The moment stretched like bubble gum. It was his opportunity, wide-open, and he didn't take it.

She gave him a soft smile—pop, moment gone—and reached for a napkin to clean herself off.

"Let me," he said gruffly, wetting another napkin from a bottle of water.

"It's fine."

"Sure, fine." He blew a raspberry at her, then ignored the pang of deja vu. Yeah, she'd done the same thing when she hadn't wanted to talk about her family stuff. Which had been fair. Here, he was being a childish weeny and he knew it. "It's actually the least I could do." He leaned over and kissed her. "And I'd like to do it. If you'd let me."

She reached up and touched his mouth, then rubbed her palm against the stubble on his jaw. "Clean up your mess, baby."

She probably hadn't meant it to be dirty, but desire surged through him at the endearment. Fuck yeah, he'd come on her skin. Made a mess and written his name in it.

He didn't deserve her, but he'd marked her anyway. And now he was going to wipe it all away, and nobody would be the wiser.

But he'd know.

And deep down, a tiny voice told him she knew, too.

The mood shifted when they headed back to camp. Not in a necessarily bad way, but he felt it—a distancing, and he wasn't sure if it was coming from him or her. He knew he didn't like it, but he also thought it was probably for the best.

They ran across Prina and Molly on their way to the lake, and when they asked Tegan if she wanted to swim, she hesitated.

"Go," he said, lifting her hand so he could kiss her knuckles. "I'm going to find a beer and chill for a bit."

"Okay." She pressed up on her toes, her gaze locked on his, but there were people around.

This was definitely not a moment for baring his soul to her.

He stood there and watched as she headed down to the boathouse. Molly had brought her a swimsuit, and they disappeared inside to change.

He still didn't move.

"How's it going, man?" He turned to find Michael Tully standing nearby, casually holding two bottles of beer. "You want one?"

"Sure." He accepted it, then twisted off the cap and tapped the bottle against Michael's. "Cheers."

"You having fun?"

"Yeah. Great place here." He was so not good with small talk. He took a long pull of beer, letting the cold

135

bubbles slide down his throat.

"Wasn't sure it would be for you when you arrived."

"That makes two of us."

"Tegan's something else, huh?"

Wyatt frowned. "What are you doing, man?"

Michael laughed. "Yeah, I'm transparent as fuck. I don't know. I just saw you looking at her, and thought, shit. That's a look I know well."

Wyatt snorted. "That makes one of us."

"I also know what it's like to stubbornly hang on to a plan, even when it's not working."

"There's nothing wrong with my plan, dude."

"That's not what I'm saying. There wasn't anything wrong with my plan, either. I was being groomed to be the CEO of my family's corporation and I was damn good at my job. I'm a businessman to my core."

"I don't follow."

"My wife. Man, nothing else matters. That plan didn't include my wife, because she didn't want any part of that world and I didn't notice until it was almost too late. And nothing else matters without her. More to the point, there's more than one life plan that fits. But there's only one mate, at least for me."

"I think you're way reaching here. I just met Tegan."

"I wasn't talking about Tegan. But your mind went

to her."

"Then what the hell were you talking about?"

Michael shrugged. "Unhappiness in general. How people need people."

Wyatt didn't fucking need anyone except his SEAL teammates.

Go find Tegan and say that to her face.

Hard, heavy guilt slammed into him and he tipped his beer back again.

Michael cleared his throat. "I shouldn't have said anything."

"I need to go."

"Heather's going to kick my ass. I'm supposed to leave the counselling to Birk."

Wyatt snorted. "All due respect to your wife, I don't want to talk to a guy named Birk about this, either."

"Then we can keep this entire exchange between us."

"Deal."

❊ ❊ ❊

Tegan watched from the dock as Wyatt talked to Michael Tully. Even from a distance she could tell he was frowning, and his body language was tense, too.

When the camp owner drifted away, and Wyatt sat

down heavily in one of the Adirondack chairs, she almost abandoned her plans to go swimming.

But he knew where she was. She'd made herself available to him, heart and soul, as much as she could and still keep a healthy perspective on what this was — and what it wasn't.

If he wanted to talk about whatever had gotten under his skin, he'd come find her. One look, one half-cocked smile, and she'd go wherever he wanted. Lie under the stars and hold his hand and just listen.

Or distract, with her mouth and body and her laugh. Whatever he wanted or needed.

She shivered and twisted away, leaping into the water.

"If you're done drooling, you want to race to the raft?" Prina asked.

"Yep. And...*go!*" Tegan laughed as her friends howled in protest, but she didn't put on the gas, and Prina won by half a body-length.

On the raft, her friends flirted with the lifeguard and talked about the talent show planned for the bonfire that night.

The next night, Wednesday, would be a formal dinner and dance in the boathouse. No bonfire. Tegan didn't know how she felt about that, but everyone else was excited.

Wyatt proven that morning that he was *not* a

dancer. She grinned to herself. He was adorably dorky when he tried to dance, though.

Maybe they could dance a few songs.

She rolled over and let the late afternoon sun warm her front, then she stood up. "Who wants to head back?"

"Not I," said Molly, deepening her voice.

Prina snickered, then added, "Nor I."

Tegan stuck her tongue out at them. "Then I will," she cried, and leapt into the water.

Man, to have a lake to swim in every day. That would be glorious.

When she got back to the dock, she found the camp director sitting cross-legged next to the ladder.

"Hey there," Heather said.

"Hey." Tegan climbed out and grabbed her towel.

"You busy?"

She looked up the hill. Wyatt had disappeared. "Nope. And for you, I'd make all the time in the world."

Heather grinned. "Just what I wanted to hear." She waited for Tegan to dry off and pull on a cover up, then pointed at the boathouse. "There's a bench back behind there where we can sit."

Interesting.

But Tegan didn't have to wait long to find out what her old mentor wanted. Heather launched right into it as soon as they sat down. "A little bird told me that you're looking for work."

"Oh."

"If this is a conversation that's way off base, just tell me to mind my own business."

"No." Tegan took a deep breath and told herself to not get excited. "I am looking for work. But not communications. Maybe something different."

"I know all about that. Any idea what you might be looking for?"

Tegan thought about it for a second. If Heather was offering her a connection or a networking opportunity, she didn't want to say the wrong thing, or head off on a wild tangent. But ever since Wyatt had asked her about what she might want to do, the skiing thing had really bounced around in her head. "It's kind of a long story."

"I've got time, too, if you want to share it."

She nodded. "Wyatt asked me what I wanted to do if I could do anything, no limits, no barriers, and I surprised myself with my answer. But the more I think about it, I think it's really something I want to cross off my bucket list."

Heather's brows knit together. "What is it?"

"Do ski patrol or the ski instructor thing for a winter. This winter, maybe. I don't know."

"That's awesome." Heather clapped her hands

together. "Yes, do it!"

"I don't know where I'd begin, and it's probably even too late for the coming season."

"Allison's boyfriend might be able to point you in the right direction. We can ask her to pass on your name."

"You'd do that for me?"

"In a heartbeat. Because..." Heather stretched out the word. "If you have a winter gig lined up, maybe I'll be able to convince you to stay here for the rest of the summer and work for me."

"What?" Tegan's pulse started to race. "Are you kidding?"

"Not at all." Heather grinned. "Michael has pointed out more than once that I'm working way too much. And we didn't come up here to still have a shitty work-life balance. I could use a Recreation Director. I'm doing that right now, on top of Camp Director, and it's too much. Plus you see how people are loving all the activities. It would be great to offer more, and really mix up what we're doing, but it needs to be someone's whole focus."

"I'm not sure I'm qualified."

Heather laughed. "Neither was I, and it's turned out just fine. Rule number one for camp is everyone should have fun. But it's more than that—we really give people something that they can't find elsewhere.

141

And I think you get that more than most."

"I do." Wow, the idea really excited her. "You know, I didn't want to make a big deal about it or anything, but yeah. I came here looking for hope. Fun, yes, but more than that."

"I think you found it, too. Am I right?"

Tegan laughed. "Well, I found something, all right. Not hope exactly. Bit more earthy than that."

Heather raised her eyebrows. "And maybe more substantial, too?"

Tegan groaned. Yes, but where did that leave her? Missing Wyatt like crazy and they hadn't even said goodbye yet. "Honestly? Maybe just more complicated."

Heather didn't reply right away.

And in the silence, Tegan felt Wyatt's presence. She twisted around, horror slicing through her. That was nothing compared to how she felt once she saw his face.

She said his name quietly, and he took a big step back. "Wait," she called out, but he was already moving fast. Not running. Striding. But his long legs could carry him a hell of a distance in a short period of time, and anger was a hell of a fuel. His shoulders hunched as she picked up her own pace, trying not to make more of a scene. Heather had seen them—Tegan had just left her on the bench behind the boathouse.

But nobody else had to see Wyatt in pain. So she resisted the urge to sprint, to catch up to him, until he disappeared into the woods.

Except when she got there, he wasn't on the path ahead of her, and by the time she got to the cabins, he was nowhere in sight.

CHAPTER THIRTEEN

Wyatt watched from the shadows as Tegan turned around in the grassy space between Cabin Eight and Cabin Nine, confusion writ all over her face.

"Wyatt!" she hollered, no longer caring about propriety. He winced, but the way his blood was pumping right now, they couldn't have this conversation.

He wasn't ready to hear that he was a complication she didn't need in her life. And he wasn't stupid—he knew that wasn't all she felt. But he'd heard enough of her conversation with Heather to understand that she had an easier option right in front of her. A smarter option than hooking her hopes and dreams to a guy that was gone more often than not.

And to think he'd been about to ask her to come out west for a bit and try to find something in California.

Like a man who adored her.

He shook his head. He needed to stay away from Tegan until he could handle saying goodbye to her in a way that didn't make it heavy.

She paced back and forth between the cabins and the path, then swore under her breath and headed up the trail toward his fishing hole.

He gave her a five minute head-start, then went

into his cabin. He grabbed a wool shirt, some packaged food, and a bottle of water. He fired a text message off to Grady that would send once he hit the high ground and caught a cell tower. Then he headed after her.

Not to catch up, though. No, Tegan would have no clue he was watching over her today.

Tonight he was going to sleep under the stars and figure out just when the fuck he'd let down his guard and let her into his heart.

❊ ❊ ❊

By the time dawn fully broke the horizon, he was awake. He'd slept like shit, and not just because he was under a tree without a blanket.

What he'd really missed was a woman.

One woman, who he'd watched head back to her cabin, tears in her eyes.

He was a fucking asshole for doing that to her, and his own hurt paled in comparison.

The walk back to camp didn't take him that long. He hadn't been that far away, just up on the high ground.

To his surprise, he found his cabin empty—except for a small, curled-up body in his bed.

He dropped to his knees next to her. "Tegan."

She blinked her eyes open—and then just stared at him.

"What are you doing in my bed?"

She rolled onto her back and stared at the ceiling. "So you're back."

"Yeah."

"And alive and in one piece."

"That wasn't really a concern."

"For you!" she yelled, suddenly loud. She pushed at him and he stumbled back, falling on his hands. She climbed out of bed and he didn't miss that she was wearing his shirt.

"Yeah, for me. And I bet Grady and Danny told you I was fine."

She nodded sharply. "They did. Not that I needed them to tell me that you're the type of guy who's most comfortable in the woods. Blah blah blah, the one thing that never changes. Do you know how scared I was?"

"I'm sorry." And he was. "I just needed to clear my head."

"Next time leave a note."

"I sent Grady a text message when I found a signal." Although his friend had probably given up trying to check his messages. It was a weak excuse. "Where are they?"

"Having a pajama party next door. We have four

beds, and Molly likes torturing Danny."

"And he likes being tortured."

"Something like that." She crossed her arms. "Look, I think I'm supposed to say sorry for what you heard yesterday, but after your vanishing act, I think we have bigger things to talk about."

He nodded. She wasn't wrong.

She paced away from him. "This is complicated. What we have. But it's also…sweet. And in balance, a good thing. You've made my week, Wyatt." She glanced back at him over her shoulder. In the early morning light, she looked innocent and fragile.

"If things were different…"

"Don't." She shook her head. "That's…I just wanted this week to be awesome. This is a serious departure from that plan, and I know it's selfish of me, but just… Don't finish that thought. Because there's no good end to that conversation, right? The next word is *but*. And I don't want to hear it, for a lot of complicated reasons. I promise I don't have any expectations. Whatever happens, happens. Let's focus the conversation there."

❀ ❀ ❀

Tegan's heart pounded in her chest. But she'd gotten that out, and survived. That was a big step.

Wyatt rocked back on his heels and crossed his arms. He was wearing a few layers of clothing, and it looked like he'd slept on the ground.

It took all of her willpower not to cross the room and hug him.

"Whatever happens, happens," he repeated, his voice rough. "And whatever doesn't happen?"

"No big deal."

"No big deal." Again with the repetition. And this time, his jaw tightened and his eyes glittered.

So he was still mad at her.

"Yes." No, she screamed inside. But she needed to be practical and not give in to a flight of fancy. Because *yes* was the right answer, even if it felt wrong.

Feelings weren't reliable.

"I—" He shook his head. "You know what? This was a mistake."

She recoiled as if he'd hit her. It was exactly what she'd feared—that somehow she wouldn't be good enough. And now because she was telling him there were no expectations, *that* wasn't good enough? Well, screw him and the high horse he stormed in on. "Clearly."

"I thought if I stayed away last night, I'd come back clear headed. But the truth is, I'm never going to be that cool around you. You..."

"I what? Do I piss you off?"

148

He just stared at her.

"Maybe that's the what it is with us." She licked her suddenly dry lips. "We grated at each other from the first moment."

"That's not the whole of it."

"But you don't deny that's what we do."

"Is it?" His face was totally hard now, unreadable and entirely closed off.

"All week…" Her voice faltered, because the words weren't quite right. But the kernel of it was true. They were nothing more than two broken people who'd rubbed against each other's raw edges for fun, at first, then found it was even more fun to just…rub against each other.

If they'd tumbled further than that, accidentally seen more of each other's soul, it had been a mistake.

Hot tears pressed against her eyelids, and this time, it was her turn to run.

❈ ❈ ❈

The boathouse was strung with tiny white Christmas lights. Tegan hadn't noticed all week, although she'd been a little distracted. And this was the first night they'd been turned on.

Heather and Michael were slow dancing in the middle of the floor. It was really adorable, but it also made her want to cry.

Again.

When she ran from Wyatt's cabin that morning, she'd let them fall freely. Instead of heading to her cabin, she'd run to the main lodge and gone in the back door.

Meg and Allison had been prepping food in the kitchen, and they took one look at her and knew exactly what she needed — Irish coffee and a giant slice of apricot cake.

And space.

They'd spirited her upstairs and stashed her in a VIP room that wasn't being used. She'd fallen asleep on the king-sized bed, and when she woke, she felt marginally better.

That only lasted until she ventured outside and saw Wyatt again, across the lawn, where he sat scowling into a cup of coffee.

Her next retreat was back to her own cabin. Molly and Prina took one look at her and started planning their revenge on the men of Cabin Nine. Tegan didn't bother to stop them.

Their revenge wouldn't touch the damage she'd already done. And Grady and Danny would protect Wyatt.

Later, she refused to go to dinner. Her friends went without her and brought back a plate of food, which she picked at while she stared, unseeingly, at a novel Prina had given her.

Finally, Molly sat beside her and clapped her on the knee. "Come back to the boathouse with us for dancing."

"No."

"Yes."

"No."

"Did it sound like a question?"

"Yes."

"Then you weren't listening very—"

"I don't want to see him." Her voice cracked and she looked down at where her hands had twisted in the blanket.

"Why not?"

"Because…"

Prina came and sat on the other side of her. "Did your camp crush turn into something more serious?"

She closed her eyes and nodded.

"Did he break your heart?"

That was a harder question to answer. She slowly shook her head. "I did that all on my own."

"Then put on a pretty dress and show him that you're just fine."

"But I'm not." Another crack in her voice. It matched the ones deep inside her chest.

Prina leaned in and pressed her forehead against

Tegan's temple. "You will be. And the first step to regaining that faith in yourself is showing *everyone* that you get back up."

The words sounded right. They felt like total shit.

But somehow she'd ended up standing on the edge of the dance floor in a sundress, true love on full display right in front of her.

She took a deep breath and pivoted, searching for the bar.

She found Wyatt instead, sitting with his back to the wall, legs sprawled out in front of him. Loosely swinging a bottle of beer by the neck.

Her gaze tangled on those long, thick fingers. Remembering what they felt like on her skin. Between her legs.

Against her cheek, gentle as anything.

And now he was lost to her, not hers at all.

They'd had three days. Amazing how much pain a short fling had managed to create in its implosion.

She dragged her gaze back to his face, then kept on going, refocusing her attention on the bar. He didn't say anything, barely even looked at her, and when she turned around after she'd ordered a drink, he was standing.

She watched in disbelief as he headed out the side door.

So much for being brave.

She grabbed her glass of wine and followed him.

There were quite a few people outside. One group had circled all the Adirondack chairs they could find. A couple was leaning against the side of the boathouse, talking quietly, the only sound spilling from them the occasional laugh.

Nobody else was on the dock, though. Just Wyatt.

She took a sip of wine and watched him.

So he hadn't really run away. The dock was boathouse-adjacent. Just the outdoor space thereof.

And he was the type who needed his space. She knew this about him. So she also knew she should turn around and go back inside.

Instead, she stood there, sipping her wine and watching.

Maybe he felt her gaze on her back. Maybe— wishful thinking—he'd been wondering if she would follow. Either way, he turned around and caught her looking.

She didn't glance away.

After a long, painful beat, he lifted his glass.

It wasn't strictly speaking an invitation, but she took it as one anyway and walked toward him.

"Haven't seen you all day," he said quietly when she stopped in front of him.

"I've been around."

"We didn't finish talking."

She shook her head. "Not fun. I veto talking."

He lifted his beer and took a sip.

She inhaled slowly, trying to control her pulse. "Nice night. Full moon."

He glanced up. "Lots of light."

"Mmm."

"What do you want bet someone goes skinny dipping tonight?"

She shrugged. Maybe.

"I dare you." He said it levelly, and it took an extra beat for it to sink in.

Her back snapped straight and rigid. "You don't get to do that."

"No?" His nostrils flared and his eyes turned steely. "Long, time-honoured camp tradition, no?"

She flailed around for an answer beyond *I don't want any more dares from you.* "It's against the rules."

"Then you don't do it now."

"I'm not doing it at all."

He paused, then made a decisive *ah* sound. "Then I win."

"Win what?"

"We're tied."

She blinked at him.

"For dares. Wyatt 2, Tegan 2. If you do this dare, you edge me out."

Oh for the love of all that was holy... "You were

154

keeping *score?* That's so unbelievably stupid."

This whole thing was stupid. Feelings, drama, boys...the whole lot of it. Ridiculous. And she was going to cry again, so she needed to go find some hard lemonade, stat.

He shrugged and tipped his beer bottle back, draining it. He stalked closer, pausing in front of her long enough to mutter, "Midnight. I dare you. Up to you."

CHAPTER FOURTEEN

There was no way she was going to show up on command at midnight and go skinny dipping for him.

But the dare had reset her feelings in a way nothing else had that day. It was, even with the angry edge to it, a little bit of the camp awesome she'd wanted so badly.

She'd do it on her own terms, though. She waited until half past eleven, and then ducked out of her cabin.

Of course Wyatt anticipated that, and he was sitting on a chair he'd pulled out onto the dock.

She stopped short of where he was. "What are you doing here?"

He stood up. "I dared you. It only counts if I'm here to confirm you actually do it."

"You came here to see me strip naked?" she asked. It was really a stupid question, and she only asked it to bait him. That's where they were at now. Back to sparring.

She hated it.

"I'll turn around."

Anger surged inside her and something snapped. "Is that what you want?"

He didn't answer her.

Damn, but he pissed her off. "Well?" she shouted,

running toward him, her arms wide. She stopped a few feet short of him and stared. "Is that what you fucking want, Wyatt?"

"I don't know," he growled back. "And keep your fucking voice down."

"Or what?" She laughed. "No such thing as camp jail."

"We don't need an audience for this." He moved closer, his entire body vibrating as he breathed audibly. He was fuming, clearly.

That made two of them. "Why not?" She raised her voice again. "Afraid people will know we cared for each other for a hot minute?"

Even in the moonlight, it wasn't hard to see his jaw flexing as he gritted his teeth. "Fine," he spit out. "Attract a crowd. I don't care." He notched his fingers into board shorts and shoved them dangerously low on his hips.

"What are you doing?"

"Point is up for grabs, woman. Either you go skinny dipping or I do."

"That's not how a dare works! You can't dare yourself to do something and you certainly aren't—"

The rest of what she was going to say didn't matter, because his shorts were on the ground and he was sprinting to the end of the dock.

Oh, but he was a handsome man.

157

And that ass.

She bit her lip and forced herself to remember they weren't on ass-ogling terms.

Well, there was only one thing to do. She pushed the straps of her sundress off her shoulders and shimmied out of it. She wasn't wearing a bra. She hesitated at the panties, but after taking a deep breath, she dropped those to the deck, too.

It was completely insane that he'd kept *score*. But there was no chance in hell she was letting him claim a point for this. That was entirely unacceptable, and she was going to tell him that in no uncertain terms, just as soon as she caught him.

She chased after him and launched herself into the dark water. The plunge into the coolness was different in the dark. She couldn't see him, even when she opened her eyes, but as soon as she broke through the surface, there he was.

The moon reflected enough light down on them that she had no problem making out the look on his face—not that she understood it. He didn't look mad anymore, at least. But there was so much about him that she'd probably never get.

How he could be so loving and such a jerk in equal measure.

Why he'd come back at her with this dare when he'd obviously just wanted to be done with her.

"What are you doing?" she asked, suddenly not sure of anything.

He shrugged. "I missed your damn race. Your stupid swim test. Let's do a do-over."

"What?"

"How does it start? Tread water for two minutes?"

"We don't have a timer."

He gave her a long, slow, disbelieving look. "I can count in my head."

"Yeah, but—"

"I need to meet timings to the tenth of a second or people die, Tegan." He splashed water at her. "But my watch also has a timer on it."

"What the—did you just *splash me*? Playfully?" She smacked the water, spraying him right back. "Fuck you and your playfulness, asshole. Set the timer."

"Two minutes?"

"Yes. And no deducting any seconds for the time we've already been in."

"Good. Gives me that much longer to look at your tits."

She growled and spun around.

He laughed, the beast. "Or your ass. I'm easy."

She turned enough that he'd have a forty-five degree angle view of hopefully nothing but curves, not that it mattered. "No fucking kidding you're easy. And crude. And totally going to lose this race."

159

He snorted and she decided it would be better to just ignore him.

Besides, he wasn't the only one who could count in his head. Maybe she couldn't do it to the tenth of a second, but she wouldn't be surprised by the beep.

And she was closer to the raft.

Tell him the cold water isn't kind to him, the part of her that felt dumped whispered.

Don't you dare cheat, the rest of her said. *And you probably dumped him.*

No, she hadn't. And nobody had been dumped. It wasn't that straightforward.

If they were in the same city—or hell, even the same state—there wouldn't be any question they'd see each other again.

Or if she was in a better place, job-wise. Life-wise.

But before she could unravel those thoughts, her competitive instincts kicked in. *Five, four, three…* and beside her, Wyatt took a deep breath. He'd been counting, too.

The beep was strangely loud on the still lake. All she could think as she dove beneath the water and kicked blindly for the raft was that Wyatt must have been holding his hand out of the water so the beep would be clearly audible.

Nice of him.

The beastly jerk.

She snarled under water and exhaled the last of the air in her lungs, the bubbles rushing past her face. Now she was just pushing insults together.

Awful lot of work, that, when she was supposed to be moving on. Good riddance and all that.

She'd kick his ass — or more likely, watch his ass as he beat her soundly, since he was definitely a better swimmer than her. And then they'd call this a draw, even-steven, and head to their respective cabins.

Maybe that's what this was.

Closure.

In the most juvenile fashion possible.

❁ ❁ ❁

Wyatt swam toward the raft. He'd already been out here at the end of the day, and he'd counted the strokes it took to get there.

He wasn't powering, though. Not as long as Tegan was just a body's length behind him.

He had to make it seem legitimate that she pass him at the end.

She'd kick his ass if he just let her win, but that was the only way he could make this work.

He sank below the surface, letting her gain a bit on him with that beat. Up, swim. Sink again. Lose a little more ground.

She'd kick his ass. But it would be worth it.

As they reached the raft, she realized she was nearly abreast of him, and turned on her motor.

He tried not to grin when her hand slapped at the raft and hit the cotton t-shirt he'd left for her.

She hauled herself in and stared at it.

He grabbed on to the raft, too, but stayed far enough away that she'd have to work to get at him for that ass kicking.

"What is this?"

"It's a shirt."

She pushed a strand of wet hair off her forehead. "Why didn't you grab it?"

Time for honesty. "It wasn't a race. You're already the team captain."

She shoved at his chest, just within pushing range. "That's not how it works."

Her hand felt good against his skin, even when she was mad. "Why not?"

"Because it's a *race*. You wanted a do-over, so we do *the thing* over again. Not a *make up your own rules* free-for-all."

"I wanted to do something else."

"What?"

"This." He pulled her tight against him, trying like hell to ignore that she was naked, and he pressed his mouth against hers.

162

She gasped, a tiny *oh* sound that hit him straight in the gut.

"I'm sorry," he whispered against her mouth. "I'm an idiot. But basically I got scared, and I thought it would be better to push you away than to tell you how I feel."

"What is happening?" She shifted in his arms, and he loosened his grip, but she didn't move away.

That was a good sign.

"I'm trying to tell you that I don't care if we're complicated."

"We really are."

"At least we're not boring."

"Wyatt…"

"I love you."

She froze, and his heart jackhammered so loud he was sure she could hear it. "What?"

"I love you. And I have very little to offer beyond that. I'm going overseas sooner than later, for quite a while. Months. I'm grumpy, especially when I'm forced to be social. I don't even have a permanent residence at the moment, because I live out of barrack's boxes and move wherever Uncle Sam wants me to go. In short, I'm not much of a catch. But from the second I heard your voice, I've been captivated by you. And if you'd let me, I'd like to court you."

The last bit didn't even sound like him, but he was

163

running on fumes now. Shit. He hadn't thought this part through. He thought he'd just give her the t-shirt and she'd be happy.

He should tell her about that part. "And I made you that t-shirt."

"Molly made these shirts." She was still blinking at him like he'd gone crazy.

"Turn it over."

She dragged her gaze away from him and flipped the t-shirt on the raft so the back was visible.

In thick black marker, he'd written **CAPTAIN**.

She stared at it for a few seconds, then made a sound in the back of her throat.

"Is it okay? I could have asked Molly to help, but she looked like she'd rather slay me than help in any way."

"It's…wow."

He reached out and circled his index finger on the curve of her shoulder. "I don't know how to do relationships. But I'm willing to try. Starting with a better attempt at talking, if you're willing."

She nodded, but still didn't look at him. Instead she chewed on her bottom lip and stared at the t-shirt.

This time, he kept his mouth shut and waited.

She tipped her head up to the night's sky, and it was only then that he realized she was silently crying.

"Oh, Tegan…"

"I'm not crying," she muttered.

"No. Of course not."

"I'm scared, Wyatt."

"Okay."

"I don't have a lot to offer right now, either. I just decided to quit my grown-up life and play college kid for a while. And I'm pathologically social, which is going to get awkward, I'm sure. But I know the feeling…"

His heart slammed into his throat as she trailed off, but when she turned her head toward him and finally smiled, a wave of palpable relief washed over him. "The feeling?"

"That crazy, out-of-control, could-this-be-love feeling. And that's scary, too, because it's way too soon."

He nodded. "Yeah. Way too soon."

She moved closer and wrapped her arms around his neck.

There was no ignoring how naked she was now. She was rubbing her naked all over his naked, and it felt too damn good.

"But that's the thing about feelings," she whispered against his lips as she rocked against him. "Kind of like dares. You just gotta roll with them and see what happens."

CHAPTER FIFTEEN

Christmas

"You have any plans for tomorrow?" Tegan's boss paper-clipped the last of the day's lesson receipts together and stuck them in an envelope. "We'd be happy to have you over for dinner."

"Thank you, that's sweet." It wasn't the first time the head of the ski school had made the offer. But Tegan wasn't in the most festive of moods. Wyatt had headed overseas in October, and they'd kept in touch as much as possible, but between her schedule once she'd arrived in Colorado, the time difference, and a weird tension that kept cropping up when they talked...it had been a few days since they'd had a really good chat.

Damn it. She'd had a plan.

Ski all winter.

Try not to miss him too much.

Head out west as soon as he got back from his deployment in the spring.

And be available all day long on Christmas Day, just in case he had a chance to call.

Now she was feeling kind of foolish for letting herself think he cared as much as she did about a stupid holiday, when where he was, nothing stopped because it was a random, arbitrary date on the calendar.

From the front entrance came the sound of the door being pulled open, a wrenching, sucking sound because the rubber seal was wet and starting to ice up on the outside.

"Crap, I forgot to lock up," Tegan said, pushing to stand, her tired legs protesting every inch of effort.

"I'll tell whoever it is that we're closed," her boss said, waving her off. "You go and clock out. It's Christmas Eve. Time to head home."

Home wasn't much. She shared a two-bedroom condo with another instructor who'd headed home to Denver for the holidays. Maybe she'd FaceTime with Molly tonight. Her friend could go to Rockefeller Plaza and show her the tree all lit up. Use the hot tub on the roof of the building and try to keep some perspective on just how good her life had been the last six months, even if she was somewhat lonely on this particular set of days.

"Tegan," her boss said, reappearing in the doorway. "Sorry. There's a guy here who's interested in booking all your available lesson time in the next few days."

She laughed. "Okay. Sure."

"He said someone dared him to learn how to downhill ski."

※ ※ ※

Wyatt was bone-tired. He'd had to take four flights to get from the Middle East to a mountain in Colorado, but when Tegan streaked out of the back office and launched herself into his arms, it was worth every hour spent crammed into last-minute economy seats.

"What are you doing here?" she whispered as she peppered his mouth with kisses. "Is everything okay? Oh my God. You look like hell. And you're so gorgeous. And here. How are you here?"

He squeezed her tight, then set his hands on her upper arms and eased her back. "I thought we might spend Christmas Day together. I've got five days of leave, basically. It's a long story. And I'll tell you the whole thing as soon as we can get out of here."

"I didn't think I'd see you until spring."

"I didn't want to get your hopes up. We get leave, but sometimes it's cancelled."

"You've been keeping secrets from me?"

"Sorry."

"You bad, bad man."

"Punish me."

"I will." She kissed him again. "But not here. Let's go."

She dragged him out to her car, an ancient 4WD he remembered she was sharing with her roommate.

"You can put your bag in the trunk, or the back seat," she babbled, and he dropped the bag in the snow, because who the fuck cared about where it went when he could kiss her in the quiet of the parking lot?

Her nose was cold and her mouth warm.

"I've missed you," he said. Understatement of the century.

"Me, too." Her voice shook. "Especially the last few days."

"Sorry about the radio silence."

"It's okay."

"Tour's halfway done. I'll be home in the spring. And we'll have some serious time together before you head back to camp."

She nodded and he kissed her again, this time harder. He wanted inside her ski suit. He wanted to strip her bare, and that couldn't happen here. He wrapped her tight in his arms and whispered how much he loved her, then picked up his bag and finally followed orders.

He settled into the passenger seat, resting his hand on her thigh as she drove the short distance to her condo.

Inside, he barely noticed the brief pointing tour she gave him as she stripped off her outerwear. All he could see was Tegan.

His Tegan.

And as the layers stripped away, for both of them, that familiar restlessness rose to the surface. The hungry tiger that never got his fill of her because they lived on opposite sides of the country—but not forever. And really, not for long.

She'd readily agreed to come to California when he returned from his tour overseas.

Now he just had to convince her to make it a permanent move.

He prowled toward her, catching her around the waist when she was down to her high-tech long-johns. "Which way to the shower?"

She laughed and pointed down the hall.

In the bathroom, they got the rest of the way naked, then she was in his arms again, his mouth on hers. Blindly, she turned on the shower, and together they stumbled under the hot spray.

She slid a slippery bar of soap into his hand and he ran it down one of her arms, then up the other. Over her shoulders, which were getting tight with new muscles. He twisted her so she was under the spray, then kissed each of those now squeaky clean spots. She returned the favour, and back and forth they went until he thought he might actually bust a nut if he didn't get inside her.

And just before he hit that *is it rude to demand to fuck your girlfriend* point, she leaned back against the tiled wall and pulled him close, one leg up around his waist, and he didn't need to wait any longer.

EPILOGUE

April

San Diego, California

Tegan walked through the arrival gate and right past luggage claim. She didn't have any suitcases with her, just her carryon bag.

Everything she owned was being shipped across the country and would arrive in a day or two, because on Christmas morning, Wyatt had made her breakfast in his boxer briefs and she'd agreed to move in with him.

There was a direct causal relationship between those two things happening, but she wasn't complaining. Even though most of their relationship had happened long distance, they'd overcome their intense, combustible start and settled into a surprisingly sweet and kind dynamic that made her happier than she'd ever imagined.

And in six weeks, she'd pack up again and fly east to spend the summer at Camp Firefly Falls as the Recreation Director—a role Heather filled the summer before, but this year she wanted some help.

It wasn't a great long-term plan, working in the Berkshires in the summer, Colorado in the winter, and finding time with Wyatt in between whenever they could.

But it was her *this year* plan. And only this year. At the end of the summer, she was coming back here for good. Back to him, for good.

Twenty-one weeks, and they'd be doing the domestic thing on a full-time basis.

If Wyatt had taught her anything, it was that everything was easier when broken down into manageable chunks of time. His six month deployment overseas had been counted down by months and weeks. Not days, not until the end. Their time apart while she wrapped up her life on the east coast was just items on a to-do list, and with each one checked off, she'd been a step closer to this moment right now.

Stepping into the California sunshine and being swept off her feet by the man she adored with her whole heart.

"Baby," she whispered as he swung her around, his face buried in her neck. "I've missed you."

"Not nearly as much as I've missed you, woman." He cupped her face and kissed her mouth hard. "You're here."

"I am."

"Can I take you home?"

She beamed at him. "You one hundred percent can."

He had a gleaming white pick-up truck parked in the lot just across the road, and before her heart stopped hammering, he was whisking her onto the freeway and around downtown. She glanced around in awe, soaking up all the ways that San Diego was different from New York. Palm trees. Amazing. And traffic wasn't insane. The entire drive to the Coronado bridge only took ten minutes, and nobody gave them the finger.

She gasped as they rose over the city, the bridge curving around and depositing them on the other side of the harbor.

She'd seen this on her computer many times, obsessively Google Street Viewing her new neighborhood.

It was totally different in person. Brighter, sunnier, happier. Way more beautiful, and she'd already been in love from afar.

When Wyatt said he had the opportunity to buy a home from a former SEAL who had mentored him, she was thrilled for him.

When he asked her to move in with him, she hadn't hesitated before saying yes.

Yes, this was her new home.

Her mother would deal. Tegan would make the most of her last summer in the Berkshires, driving to see her mother while still within reasonable distance to do so, and her mother was coming to camp for what Heather was secretly calling Silver Fox week.

But she didn't need to think about that for six weeks.

She grinned across the truck cab at Wyatt, who looked so good she could take a bite out of him.

Without taking his eyes off the road, he reached over and squeezed her thigh. "Almost there."

He turned left, then right, weaving into the residential neighborhood. All the houses were beautiful and unique—and small. He hadn't been kidding about that part when they'd talked on the phone. Somehow they looked bigger in photos. But space was at a premium.

Finally he stopped in front of a small bungalow. She couldn't take it all in, but she tried. Oh, she tried.

"It's not much," he said as he swung the door open. "And I haven't started unpacking."

She moved past him into the small, sunlight front room of their new house.

And she burst into tears.

It was perfect.

"Tegan," he groaned, wrapping his arms around her from behind. "No, sweetie, don't cry."

"They're good tears," she sniffled. "This is our home."

He nodded against her hair. "It is."

"I never imagined…" She blinked, and it was still there. The gleaming wood floors and the freshly painted walls. Warm butter yellow, white trim. A stack of boxes scrawled with Wyatt's handwriting. **Books** on one of them. **Living room junk** on the other two.

She started giggling. "Living room junk?"

"Probably should have just tossed that shit," he grumbled.

She wriggled out of his arms and walked across the room. She loved this man with her whole heart, but she had no clue what kind of *junk* he might have in his living room.

Inside the top box she found a bunch of CDs, a stack of photo albums, and a couple of heavier objects wrapped in newspaper. Ceramic sculptures? She pulled back the newspaper and laughed out loud. "Is that an army helmet?"

"Yeah. From the first world war." Again he moved closer, settling his arm on her hip, and she leaned against him. "It doesn't need to go out here. There's a sunroom I can put a display shelf up in."

"It's fine." She breathed in, then exhaled happily. "Wow. This is really happening."

He cupped her cheek, his thumb carefully tracing her lower lip as he searched her face. "I'm so happy you're here. I love you."

"I love you, too." She parted her lips and let her

tongue trace the edge of his thumb. "Continue the tour? Where's our bedroom?"

He grinned. "That's the one room I took the liberty of setting up before you got here."

"You did?" She stepped around him, suddenly curious.

The kitchen was next, then a short hallway, with a bathroom and two bedrooms. One was empty.

The other had a big-ass king sized bed, with bedding that was suspiciously familiar.

"Is that from camp?"

She whirled around to find him leaning against the door frame with a pleased grin on his face. "It is."

The night they'd gone skinny dipping, she'd snuck him into the empty VIP suite in the main lodge and they'd finally slept together—under the blanket that now graced their bed in California.

"Did you have to fess up to Heather about why you wanted it?"

He laughed. "I called Michael. Man to man. I don't know what he told his wife, but the bedding showed up a week later with a matching pair of mason jar mugs. They're the only dishes in our kitchen right now."

"Oh, baby." She pressed her hands to her chest. "I love it."

"And there's one more thing," he said as he moved

closer.

"What?" The backs of her legs bumped into the bed as he crowded into her before lifting her up and laying her flat on her back.

"I was thinking about how you said this was your last summer at camp coming up."

"It is. I promise."

"Okay. But I was thinking we could go back together next year."

"Really?" She gave him a giant smile. "I'd love that."

"On one condition."

"Anything."

He braced his arms on either side of her and kissed her slowly and thoroughly. "The wedding planning can't take over our lives. You're limited to one weekly wedding discussion of no more than thirty minutes."

She froze.

He grinned. Then he trailed a fingertip over her chest and up into the space between their faces. On his first knuckle was a gorgeous emerald ring. "I dare you to marry me."

RETURN TO CAMP FIREFLY FALLS

Thank you for reading this story! *Skinny Dipping Dare* is one of many romances set at Camp Firefly Falls. Visit our website at www.campfireflyfalls.com to discover all the stories!

Coming up next in this series from me… Prina returns to camp for a much needed week of solitude. But a certain Navy SEAL wants to discuss the unfinished—and very secret—fling they had last summer. Look for *Take a Chance on Me* in Summer 2017.

~ Zoe
www.zoeyork.com

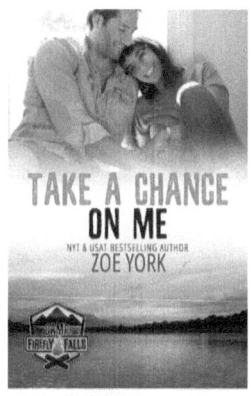

www.ingramcontent.com/pod-product-compliance
Lightning Source LLC
Chambersburg PA
CBHW030255130626
46549CB00002B/546

* 9 7 8 1 9 2 6 5 2 7 4 3 7 *